Sweet bunny rabbit?

Jackie eavesdropped openly on the one-way conversation. The caller was obviously a boy. Only a boy could turn her surly sister into a sweet bunny rabbit. Instead of her usual sharp laughs, Sharon emitted a dainty new laugh, like she was nibbling on a piece of expensive chocolate. Jackie practiced the dainty laugh, wondering how Sharon could keep up the breathy voice much longer without passing out. Her chest felt like she had just had a bad attack of hiccups. After an oozy good-bye, Sharon hung up.

"Who was that?" Jackie cooed.

"Were you here the whole time?" Sharon screamed in her regular old voice. "You're history, Jackie!"

Coming soon by
CANDICE F. RANSOM
in Apple Paperback:

My Sister, the Traitor
My Sister, the Creep

MY SISTER THE MEANIE

Candice F. Ransom

AN
APPLE
PAPERBACK

SCHOLASTIC INC.
New York Toronto London Auckland Sydney

ISBN 0-590-44116-7

12 11 10 9 8 7 6 5 4 3 2 1   0 1 2 3 4 5/9

Printed in the U.S.A.   28

For my sister,
who isn't quite so
mean any more

Chapter 1

"They wear pink on Thursdays and have this special meeting during lunch," Jackie Howard said, drawing her legs close to her chest so she could examine the scratch on her knee.

"They won't let anyone sit at their table who isn't a member. Natalie and I tried to eavesdrop at the next table, but Angel makes everybody talk in whispers. We couldn't hear a thing."

"Is that so?" Mrs. Howard spoke in the tone she used when she wasn't really paying attention. One time years ago, Jackie tested her mother by coloring a picture of a Christmas tree all black. When she showed it to her mother, who was busy fooling with something on the stove the way she was now, Mrs. Howard barely glanced at it and said, "Isn't that nice."

Jackie considered testing her again. She could go on about Angel Allen's club, the hottest group in seventh grade, and then casually mention that her mother's tea towel was on fire. It wasn't, of course, but it would be interesting to see her mother jump. Still, that was the crummy sort of thing Sharon would do.

Lifting one corner of the Band-Aid, Jackie rattled on about her favorite subject. She loved to talk, whether anyone was listening or not. "Angel had these special pink pencils made with the club's name printed in silver. Each member gets a pencil. Angel ordered a dozen pencils, and she's given out ten. There's room in her club for two more."

Angel Allen sat next to Jackie in ESG, which was a combination of English, social studies, and guidance. All seventh-graders had to take ESG. For two and a half hours every day, Jackie watched Angel take notes with her special pink pencil, the silver letters flashing under the fluorescent lights. She listened to the soft, privileged whisper of Angel's pencil and imagined belonging to Angel's exclusive club. If only she and her best friend Natalie could get in, life at Sidney Lanier Junior High would be a breeze.

"Stop picking at that scab." Her mother's voice cut through her daydream.

Absorbed in her thoughts, Jackie had peeled the Band-Aid off entirely. "I'm not picking at it. I'm just looking." The scratch was healing okay. She'd probably live to have Sharon's cat attack her again.

"What's the name of this famous club?" her mother asked. Jackie almost fell off the chair. So she was listening!

"It's called the We Like Boys Club. Angel only

lets the coolest girls join." Which was why she and Natalie didn't stand a gnat's chance of getting in.

"We Like Boys Club?" Mrs. Howard echoed. "What kind of a club is this, Jackie?" Now she was really interested.

"It's just these girls that go around," Jackie replied. "They go to the movies and roller-skating and have slumber parties and stuff."

"What about the boys part?" her mother wanted to know. "This girl sounds boy-crazy."

"She is. That's why she started the club. They talk about guys, which ones they think are cute and so on. I think the name of the club is dumb. The main reason Natalie and I want to get in is because of all the neat things the girls do."

"It doesn't sound much like my club," Mrs. Howard said.

Jackie was certainly glad of that. Her mother's women's club met at each other's houses and raised money for charities. When the club was at the Howard's house, they ate supper early, then Jackie and Sharon filled the swan dishes with butter mints and cashews. Sharon smacked Jackie every time Jackie swiped a mint and Jackie told on Sharon every time Sharon snitched a cashew. If the girls were *good*, a condition that was getting more difficult to meet, they were allowed to stay for the games. But even the games were boring. Mrs. Howard would parade around holding a tray with a bunch of objects on it like a hairbrush, a knife, four rubber bands, etc., and the players were supposed to write down as many things as they could remember.

Or they would guess the number of beans in a jar, beans that Jackie had laboriously counted out earlier.

"I don't know why I'm telling you about Angel's club," Jackie said, feeling gloomy all of a sudden. "She'll never let me join. Or Natalie either."

"Why not?"

"Oh, Natalie's not cool enough, I guess. And I'm too young." This was a particularly sore point with her.

"What do you mean too young? I thought you said Angel was in your class? Isn't she twelve like you and Natalie?"

"Yeah, but — " It was hard to explain. Jackie was the same age as most of the kids in seventh grade, but she *felt* a lot younger. She always seemed the youngest, even when she wasn't. She must have been *born* young, or had some deficiency. Having Sharon for an older sister didn't help.

Sharon was always calling her bawlbaby and Mama's baby, which was bad enough. But lately, Sharon was just plain mean. She didn't let Jackie come within twenty feet of her room or touch any of her things on pain of death.

Jackie said simply, "I just have to get in Angel's club. I won't have any fun in school this year if I don't." She sure wasn't having fun at home any more, not with Sharon the Terrible.

"School doesn't always have to be fun."

"It usually *isn't*." Except maybe for Sharon. A junior at Fairfax High, Sharon was pretty and popular. She had loads of friends and one boyfriend after the other. She was involved in all

4

sorts of interesting activities at school, like the drill team. Jackie was feverishly jealous of Sharon's drill team uniform, a short jumper with a flared skirt.

Her mother must have been reading her thoughts. "If you're comparing yourself to Sharon again, remember she's older and there are more things to do in high school. You'll have your turn, Jackie."

She doubted it. The fun stuff that Sharon did seemed to have a way of disappearing by the time it was Jackie's turn. Like field trips. When Sharon was in the third grade and Jackie was still fingerpainting at home, Sharon went on a wonderful class trip to Williamsburg. Jackie couldn't wait to start school so she could go to neat places. But by the time Jackie came along, students were no longer permitted to take trips so far outside the county. Jackie's solitary field trip experience was a two-mile train ride, in reverse. A train backing to Alexandria was hardly her idea of a glamorous excursion.

Since the prospect of a field trip or making majorettes was dim at best, Jackie absolutely had to get into Angel's club. "It's my only hope," she moaned, nearly overcome with despair.

"I wouldn't worry too much about it," her mother said, clearly tired of Angel and her club.

Jackie stretched her bare leg out in front of her, already thinking of something else. Was it time for her to shave? Her leg was covered with a kind of peach-fuzzy down. Sharon shaved her legs every five minutes, but the hair on her sister's legs was stiff and bristly. Sharon had her own electric razor. Mrs. Howard told Jackie that she would get one, too, when she turned fifteen. Jackie strongly suspected she'd wind up with Sharon's old razor, which would be so dull and worn-out by then, she'd be better off plucking the hairs out with tweezers.

"Tell your sister it's her turn to set the table," Mrs. Howard said.

Jackie really hated to tell her sister to do anything these days. But she got up and went through the living room back to the bedrooms leading off the short narrow hall. A big sign was taped to Sharon's door: DON'T TOUCH MY ROOM!

Of course the sign didn't apply to their parents, although once Sharon practically had her mother arrested for not knocking. The sign was meant for Jackie.

Jackie knocked, dreading her mission. She could hear Sharon's television blaring an old *Dick Van Dyke Show* re-run.

"Go away!"

"Mama says for you to come set the table," Jackie yelled through the door.

No sound except the laugh track from the television.

"Did you hear me?" Jackie said, louder.

The door was flung open then, so suddenly Jackie nearly toppled over the threshold from the force of in-drawn air.

Sharon stood there, globs of Noxema dotting her chin and forehead. She always dabbed the cream on her face the instant she felt a bump coming on. Even with white gunk on her face, Sharon was still pretty.

People said that the sisters looked alike, though Jackie didn't think so. Sure, they both

6

had brown eyes and brown hair, but the resemblance ended there. Sharon's hair was long and glossy and she had the longest eyelashes imaginable. Jackie had short stubby hair, short stubby fingers, and short stubby eyelashes. It was as if Mother Nature started giving Jackie everything Sharon had, but either ran short or got bored halfway through the job.

"What do you want?" Sharon snapped, pleasant as a crocodile.

"You have to set the table. Mama said."

"I heard you the first time. Now what do you *want?*"

Jackie didn't have an answer to that. If Sharon had heard her than why did she open the door? Was she worried that Jackie might contaminate her room just by standing outside?

"We're having fried potatoes tonight," Jackie offered. Sharon was a fool for fried potatoes. If the two of them ate supper alone, as they did when their father worked at his part-time job two nights a week, Sharon would pretend a spider lurked over Jackie's head, then swipe her potatoes. Now Sharon didn't bother with such deception — she simply stole Jackie's potatoes right off her plate.

"Yippee." Sharon went back to her clothes-littered bed, actually leaving the door open in Jackie's presence. Her cat Felix blinked, yellow-eyed and baleful, from his nest in Sharon's bathrobe. Sharon flopped down among the balled-up blankets and clean underwear Mrs. Howard had washed that day, and stared at her geometry book. Geometry looked tough. Jackie dreaded the day she'd be a high school junior and would have to take it. But high school was still two years away.

She ventured into her sister's room, marveling at all the neat things Sharon had that she didn't. The new furniture, the bright scatter of lipsticks and eye shadow covering the vanity top, the fake wooden "rifle" Sharon twirled in her drill team routines.

Sharon's room glaringly pointed out that Sharon was Somebody and Jackie was a Big Nothing. Jackie still had all her old Golden Books in the bookcase her father had made. No wonder Angel and the others thought she was a baby.

"Jackie — " Sharon's tone was thick and gooey all of a sudden, like a butterscotch sundae.

Jackie tensed. Whenever Sharon became sugary, Jackie had to watch out. "What?"

"Would you set the table for me tonight?"

"I did it last night. It's your turn! I'll have to do it again tomorrow and that's three nights in a row!"

Immediately Sharon's niceness evaporated, like water sucked into sand. "Well, if you're going to be so hateful about it, then forget it," she said, sounding haughty and injured at the same time. "But don't come crawling to me when *you* want a favor."

Actually, Jackie did want a favor. She was dying to borrow Sharon's pink sweater vest to wear to school on Thursday. That was the day Angel's club wore pink. If she and Natalie wore pink, too, Angel might get the idea to let them join.

But if she set the table and then asked to borrow Sharon's sweater, Sharon would know

8

Jackie had an ulterior motive. The only way to get on Sharon's good side was to act like she was thrilled to do her a favor and then, days or even weeks later, casually mention that Sharon owed *her* a favor.

Only she didn't have days or weeks to wait for Sharon to be suitably softened up. She needed the sweater vest by the next day at the latest. "All right," she relented. "I'll set the table for you." It was much too soon, but she recklessly plunged ahead. "I'll do it if you promise to lend me your pink sweater vest. I'd like to wear it to school Thursday."

"What?" Sharon bellowed, outraged.

"Your pink sweater? Can I borrow it for one day? Not even a whole day," she bargained. "I won't wear it on the bus, and I'll take it off right after ESG. . . ." Her voice trailed off.

"Forget it. Forget the whole deal. I'll set the table myself." Sharon got out of bed again, dragging the bedclothes with her knees. "And you keep your hands off my stuff."

Jackie was desperate. "I'll set the table for you every night for a whole week. A month! The rest of my life! Please let me wear your sweater, Sharon. Please!"

"I said forget it." Sharon sat down at her vanity table and wiped gobs of Noxema off with a tissue. Their mother had a fit if Sharon came to the table with Noxema smeared all over her face. "I'm going to wear that sweater myself on Thursday. I'd planned to all along."

"You weren't! You're just doing this to be mean! I'm telling!"

"Go ahead," Sharon said loftily, smiling at her

9

own reflection in the round mirror over the vanity. "Run bawling to Mama, like you always do. Crybaby, crybaby!"

Jackie was so angry at her sister that tears sprang to her eyes. She squinched them back, refusing to give her sister the satisfaction of seeing her cry.

Jackie knew that Sharon had no intention of wearing the sweater on Thursday. She probably didn't even know where it *was*, her room was such a wreck. She wasn't going to let Jackie borrow it out of sheer spite and Jackie couldn't do a thing about it.

Sharon hadn't always been so mean. There were times — maybe even three or four that Jackie could recall — when Sharon had actually been fairly decent. Jackie and Sharon used to do things together. In the summer they shared the big hammock in the shady part of their backyard, reading *Mad* magazine and comic books or taking turns hosing each other down. When school was out, there wasn't much to do in the rural area where they lived, and they relied on each other for company.

But the past summer, Sharon changed. All she wanted to do was bake in the sun and whine about living in the sticks. She scorned Jackie's comic books as too childish for words. And she wouldn't tell anybody why she was so grouchy. When Jackie asked her mother what Sharon's problem was, Mrs. Howard replied, "Growing up." Jackie didn't believe that was it — Sharon was already grown up, mostly.

Sharon's attitude didn't improve in August when she got new bedroom furniture: a bureau, a vanity with a tufted stool and a round mirror, and a bed with a white vinyl headboard. Jackie inherited Sharon's old bed with the letters S-H-A-R carved in the scarred headboard, the dresser with the broken slat in the bottom drawer, and the nightstand with the fossilized chewing gum stuck to the knob.

Naturally Jackie complained to her mother. "How come I don't get new furniture? It's bad enough I have the smallest room."

"Because you don't need new furniture," Mrs. Howard had replied, as if that were any reason. "Sharon's old things are still perfectly good."

"Good enough for *me*, you mean." Even though Jackie's old stuff was practically falling apart, she didn't want Sharon's hand-me-down junk, either.

Mrs. Howard saw the sour look on Jackie's face. "When Sharon leaves home, you can move into her room. Then you can have her furniture."

"It won't be new then." Not the way Sharon took care of her belongings.

Now Jackie dredged up her mother's promise. "Mama said when you leave, I get to have your room. And your furniture, too."

"I'd rather burn my stuff first than let you have it," Sharon declared.

"What you don't burn will have to be fumigated!"

Sharon pushed Jackie out of her room. The DON'T TOUCH MY ROOM sign fluttered as she slammed the door.

"You still have to set the table," Jackie said. "And I'm not helping you, either."

"I hate you."

11

"I hate you more!" Jackie retaliated, determined to have the last word. But Sharon had already flounced out to the kitchen, wafting the scent of Noxema and Bluegrass cologne.

If she didn't get in Angel Allen's club, Jackie would remain a Big Nothing in seventh grade. But how could she ever expect to impress an important Somebody like Angel Allen, when she was a Big Nothing in her own house?

Chapter 2

Miss Dale erased the social studies assignment from the board, signaling the fifteen-minute break before guidance.

"I don't know why we have guidance after two hours of English and social studies," Natalie McEvoy grumbled. "I don't need guidance. I'm perfectly normal. Trade purses?"

Jackie handed over her purse. It was Sharon's old vinyl clutch bag from the year before. Sharon bought herself a real leather purse, grandly bestowing her old pocketbook on her little sister like a duchess giving a penny to the scullery maid.

"Want some gum?" Natalie passed her lumpy denim purse to Jackie. "There's a brand-new pack in there somewhere."

Natalie loved to trade purses. Last week when they traded for a whole day, Natalie complained that Jackie's purse was too dull, that there wasn't anything interesting in it. Natalie's purse bulged with neat stuff like gum and Pixy Stix, makeup, a brush that held hair spray in the handle, even a snake-bite kit. "You never can tell when Daryl Forshay will lose control," Natalie had remarked, referring to a nerdy blond boy in their class who was forever saying "Cowabunga!"

Taking Natalie's criticism to heart, Jackie reorganized her purse. The first step from a Big Nothing to Somebody, she decided, was carrying around an interesting purse.

"I see you finally fixed up your wallet." Natalie thumbed through the photos of rock stars Jackie had cut out of magazines and inserted in the plastic holders. "But what's this for?" She held up a *Golden Guide to Birds*.

Jackie blushed. The only reason she had stuck the guidebook in her purse was because it fit so neatly, right next to her wallet. Also, she liked to look at the pictures. "I thought maybe I'd need it for biology," she fibbed, not wanting Natalie to think she was weird.

"The only thing you need for biology is a pillow and blanket," Natalie said. "Mrs. Wood is so *boring*. The kids in Mrs. Nicely's class say she throws peanuts at them when they take tests. She's funny."

"She's also a hard grader. She cracks jokes the whole time she's giving you an F."

"Maybe if Mrs. Wood threw peanuts at us we'd be able to stay awake."

Natalie was Jackie's friend, but not her best-best friend. Jackie had never really had a best-best friend, the kind you share everything with, both in school and out of school. It was the out

14

of school part that kept Jackie from having a close friendship. Where she lived you had to have your mother drive you if you wanted to go any place. Most of the other kids who went to Lanier lived in subdivisions. They could walk to each other's houses or to the 7-Eleven for a Slurpee. Walking to the 7-Eleven, Jackie believed, made a person cool and self-assured, like Natalie. She could tell Natalie was self-assured the instant she met her.

Jackie remembered that on the first day of junior high, she had been sitting by herself at a lab table in homeroom. A bright-faced girl with medium-length brown hair paused by the empty chair next to her.

"Anybody sitting here?" the girl asked.

Jackie shook her head. As kids filed in and claimed seats, she was beginning to think no one would sit next to her.

The girl plopped her notebook down on the slate-covered table. Jackie noticed she had tiny, dark freckles across her nose, as if they had been drawn on with a sharp eyebrow pencil. "I thought I'd never find this room. Some jerk gave me the wrong directions. My name's Natalie McEvoy. I just moved here from Seattle."

Jackie strained to remember which state Seattle was in. A blank map of the United States popped into her head. Seattle was in one of those upper-left hand corner squares, Oregon or maybe Montana. She had once put down Chicago as a state on a geography quiz. Even when her teacher corrected her, Jackie still thought Chicago seemed more important than Illinois and ought to be its own state.

"I'm Jackie Howard," she said at last, hoping Natalie would tell her where Seattle was before she slipped and said the wrong thing. "I've lived here all my life."

"In Virginia? In the same house?"

"Mostly." Jackie wondered why this was so hard for Natalie to believe.

It turned out Natalie's father was a captain in the army, and their family moved around a lot. Besides Seattle, Natalie had lived in California, Texas, and Germany.

"I've never been anywhere," Jackie said, which was the truth. She had never even scaled the Washington Monument, and that was only twenty-five miles from her house. Sharon had been to Williamsburg and once spent the weekend with a friend in West Virginia, but the only place Jackie had ever been was Alexandria, on a train running backward.

She was surprised that someone like Natalie would want to be her friend. She admired Natalie's freckles and her worldliness, but most of all she admired Natalie's courage. Natalie McEvoy didn't let junior high faze her. Jackie knew from orientation that junior high would be very different from elementary school. She didn't mind changing classes or dressing out for p.e. What Jackie hated was that she didn't know a soul. Because Jackie's house was located right on the boundary line, her old friends from Centreville Elementary went to Robert Frost Junior High instead of Sidney Lanier.

Natalie didn't know a soul either, coming from Seattle, but she had no problem striking up conversations with complete strangers. Once someone started talking to Jackie she was okay, but she could no more open her mouth and introduce herself the way Natalie did that first day than skate in the Ice Capades. The only thing Natalie couldn't conquer with brashness was Angel Allen's club.

Now Natalie finished checking out Jackie's purse and handed it back across the aisle. "How come you didn't wear pink today? It's Thursday. We were both supposed to wear pink so we'd look like we belong in you-know-who's club." Natalie had on a pink party dress with a low sash.

Jackie made a face. "Sharon wouldn't let me borrow her pink sweater vest. She said she wanted to wear it herself but she was just being mean."

"Well, maybe she'll let you borrow it next Thursday."

"Are you kidding? She'd sooner bury that sweater in the backyard than let me have it." Natalie didn't understand what it was like having a mean sister. In Natalie's family she was the oldest and nobody bossed her around.

"I'd lend you something of mine, but this is the only pink outfit I own."

In the next row, Angel Allen and Marcia Rivett, her closest friend, whispered and giggled. They both wore pink, reminding Jackie of an ad for bubble bath. There were eight other members in Angel's We Like Boys Club, from different classes. All the girls lived in the same development. Jackie had seen them walking to school in a tight cluster with Angel at the center.

Angel was even more worldly than Natalie.

17

Her skirt was the shortest in the class, and she had on pink eye shadow to match her top. Angel looked good in pink, and she knew it. She had long, perfectly straight, honey-colored hair, parted in the middle and falling in two panels on either side of her face. Two Scotty barrettes, the kind little kids wore, anchored the silky curtains out of Angel's eyes. Only Angel could wear a miniskirt with little kid barrettes and get away with it.

The two extra pink pencils, with the club's name in silver, were in plain sight in the plastic zippered bag attached to Angel's notebook. If Jackie had one of those pencils, she could sit at Angel's special table in the cafeteria and have a place saved for her at the mirrors in the p.e. locker room. It would be so wonderful to belong.

Miss Dale rapped her ruler to get the class to settle down again. "Break's over," she said. "Let's be quiet. Daryl, in your seat. *Your* seat, not Robert's. We're starting a special unit in guidance." She tugged a long yellow box from the bottom of the supply cupboard.

Daryl Forshay leaped up to help her with it. "Cowabunga! This thing weighs a ton."

"Thank you, Daryl. Just put it on that table, please."

"What, no tip?" He shook his blond bangs out of his eyes and grinned, revealing railroad-track braces.

The other girls swooned over Donnie Roebuck, the best-looking guy in seventh grade, but for Jackie, Donnie was totally unattainable. Secretly she liked Daryl, even if he was a pain.

The yellow box was just the beginning. Next,

18

Miss Dale rolled in a library cart loaded with books. Then she passed out a three-page ditto.

When Jackie received her copy of the ditto, her heart sank with dismay. It was a questionnaire on what she wanted to be when she grew up.

"We're going to be spending several weeks exploring vocational possibilities, what you want to do when you graduate from school," Miss Dale explained. "Some of you already know what you want to be. That's good. You can learn the requirements for your chosen field, even what colleges you might want to attend. For those of you who don't have any idea what you want to do, here is a chance to look over many professions to help you decide."

Natalie whispered across the aisle, "I'm going to be a vet."

Jackie studied the form, her stomach tightening. On it were questions like "Am I aware of an outstanding talent?" and "Do I like to work alone or with other people?" At the end on the third page was the statement *At this time, my choice of occupation is*, followed by a thick black line. Natalie was already writing "vetnarien" on the blank line. Probably everybody in the whole class knew what they wanted to do, except Jackie.

Miss Dale outlined their assignment. Besides filling out the questionnaire, they were supposed to write a report on the occupation they chose.

"This resource library should cover all your needs," she concluded. "The yellow box contains a folder on just about every profession there is."

"How about mortician?" Daryl, of course.

Miss Dale didn't bother to answer him. "Take only one folder at a time, please. If that job doesn't interest you, put it back in the yellow box and choose another. If you want a particular folder that someone else is using, read through these career books until the folder is returned to the box."

Before the last words were out of her mouth, the entire class stampeded to the front of the room. Jackie hung back. Might as well let the others get the folders they wanted. Someone bumped into her, and she stepped back to let the person pass. Angel Allen smirked in triumph as she clutched a red-tabbed folder marked Actor/Actress. Naturally, Angel would nab the glitziest job in the box.

"I got it!" Natalie waved her precious Veterinarian folder. "What are you hunting for?"

"I'm waiting till the crowd thins out. Who can see anything in this mob?"

Soon there were only two people around the yellow box, Jackie and a boy named Robert Labson.

"You go ahead," Robert said politely.

"No, you were here first." Jackie really wanted to be last. She didn't want Robert to watch her fumble through the folders and find out how unambitious and untalented she was.

"Well, if you insist." He pushed up the sleeves of his gray cardigan sweater and began flipping through the folders. "The others got all the good ones." He selected a folder. "This'll do, I guess."

Jackie read the blue-tabbed title. "Pharmacist?

You want to be a pharmacist when you grow up?"

"I doubt it."

"If you don't like that job, Miss Dale said you can pick another."

He shrugged. "This one's okay. I just want to get the report over with."

When he went back to his seat, Jackie riffled through the folders. Surveyor. Dietitian. Forest Ranger. They all sounded horrible.

Miss Dale came over. "Need some help, Jackie?"

"No. I mean, I don't see my job in here," she lied.

"Which one is it?" Miss Dale asked. "It might be under another category."

"It's — uh—" Desperately she tried to think of a job she knew wouldn't be in the box. Maybe Miss Dale would excuse her from writing the report and filling out that awful questionnaire. Then she remembered the guide book in her purse. She had leafed through it that morning on the bus. There was a name for scientists who studied birds. She could see it in her mind but she couldn't pronounce it. "It starts with an O."

"An O?" Miss Dale frowned. "Ocean-ographer?"

Jackie shook her head. "Orni — something."

"Orthodontist?"

"No, it's somebody who works outside. In the trees." She struggled with the elusive term. "Orni . . . orni-thia-logist."

Miss Dale stared at her. "I don't think you know what you're talking about, Jackie. Take this one. It's about a job in the trees."

She handed Jackie the Forest Ranger folder. Jackie returned to her desk, crushed with humiliation. Miss Dale probably thought she was the dumbest kid in the class! Trying to pick a job she couldn't even say right!

Natalie sneaked a peek at Jackie's folder. "Is that what you're going to be when you grow up?"

"I don't know," she said. "I'm not sure."

"If you can't think of anything, ask Sharon to help you," Natalie suggested.

Sharon! Her sister screamed like a wounded cougar if Jackie asked her the time of day. A lot of help *she'd* be.

When Jackie got home from school, Sharon was lying on the couch like Cleopatra, watching *The Milt Grant Show*, a local dance program. Her hair was in brush rollers which, over the years, had dug a hole in the armrest. "Turn it up, will you?"

"Who was your servant last year?"

"You were."

"I've been your servant since the day I was born."

"What else are kid sisters good for?" Sharon got up to fix the television herself.

Jackie spotted the empty Oreos bag on the coffee table. One lone cookie lay on a plate. That hog Sharon had eaten them all! While her sister's back was turned, Jackie took a huge bite of the cookie, to get even with Sharon for not lending Jackie her pink sweater.

Sharon spied the bite immediately. "You ate my cookie!"

"How did you know it was me? It could have been a ghost."

"I'd recognize your rat bites anywhere!"

Jackie closed her mouth. She was very self-conscious about her front teeth, which lapped over slightly. Her bites *were* distinctive, vee-shaped, like a rodent's. "It's all your fault my teeth are crooked," she said. "You pushed me when I was sitting on the table that time and made my teeth hit the windowsill."

The marks were still imprinted in the wood, vee-shaped proof that Sharon had shoved Jackie.

"Your teeth were *already* crooked when I pushed you," Sharon said. "So stop trying to blame me for your deformities."

Jackie stomped into her room, tossing her books on her bed. She could never win over Sharon! Never! The vocation form slipped out of her notebook and the final question glared up at her. At this time, what Jackie wanted to be more than anything else in the world was an only child.

Chapter 3

"I've been thinking," Natalie said at lunch one day. "About Angel's club."

"What about it?" From where she sat, Jackie could see Angel and her friends at their special table right next to the eighth-graders side. Normally, the eighth-graders stayed as far from lowly seventh-graders as they could, claiming the little kids ruined their appetites, but Angel's group seemed to be accepted by them.

"They seem older than the rest of us. Like they're at least fourteen, maybe fifteen."

"That's because Angel does things we aren't allowed to yet," Jackie pointed out. "She wears eye shadow."

"But most of the kids in seventh grade act like *kids*." She jerked her thumb toward the end of their table. "Those two winners, for instance."

Daryl Forshay and Robert Labson were horsing around. Just as Jackie was about to take a bite of her peanut butter and banana sandwich, Daryl pulled rubber erasers off the ends of two pencils and rammed one up each nostril. He grinned at her.

Natalie snorted in disgust. "Hopelessly immature."

Jackie agreed, but she still thought Daryl was cute. Right now, though, he looked pretty gross with erasers up his nose.

Daryl swiveled around to make sure everybody in the cafeteria saw him. Robert was laughing and attracting more attention.

"Angel and her crowd don't do dumb things," Natalie said. "Which is why the eighth-graders let them sit there. Her club has class."

Jackie pondered their dubious status a moment. "We don't stick erasers up our noses, either, but Angel still hasn't asked us to be in her club."

Natalie peeled her orange. "She would if *we* acted older."

"How much older?" This sounded even harder than the vocation project in ESG.

"We could probably fake acting like eighth-graders. But we want Angel to notice us this time. So let's go for acting *really* older. Like seniors."

"Seniors! Oh, Natalie, do we have to?" Jackie wished her friend had come up with a simpler task. She was having enough trouble figuring out how seventh-graders were supposed to behave.

"What've we got to lose?"

The scent of Natalie's orange was making Jackie dizzy. Or maybe it was the impossible assignment of acting like seniors. Then she remembered the Forest Ranger folder Miss Dale had chosen for her. If twelve wasn't too soon to decide what she wanted to be when she grew up, then what would it hurt to jump ahead five years? Acquiring a little senior polish might save her from spending the rest of her life in a fire tower.

"Okay," she replied weakly. "What do we have to do? Drive to school? Learn trigonometry?"

"Don't be ridiculous. Acting like a senior is more than just tough courses and a driver's permit," Natalie maintained, as if she were an expert on the subject. "It's an *attitude*. We need a role model. Somebody we can copy, so we get it down right."

"I don't know any seniors."

"But you know a *junior*, and that's the next best thing."

"Sharon, a role model? For what, a porcupine?"

"Your sister's perfect, the way she goes around like a prom queen," Natalie said. "Just ask her to give us a few pointers on how we can get that confident."

Ask Sharon, the meanest sister in the world, to help two seventh-graders act like high-school seniors? Not if she wanted to see another Christmas. The direct approach never worked with Sharon. But if Sharon didn't *realize* she was a role model. . . .

"I'll spy on her," Jackie said finally. "And copy everything she does. Then you can copy from me."

Natalie nodded, satisfied. "We should be acting like seniors in a couple of days. A week at the most."

A hand snaked out from behind Natalie's chair, reaching for the last section of her orange. Daryl Forshay clamped the orange wedge between his teeth, like the wax lips the stores sold around Halloween.

"Ladies and jellybeans!" he announced, the orange slice falling out the instant he opened his mouth. "I come before you to stand behind you to tell you something I know nothing about!"

Angel Allen and Marcia Rivett looked over at them. The word "juvenile" floated over the cafeteria noise. Jackie hoped Angel didn't think she and Natalie had anything to do with Daryl's shenanigans.

Natalie rolled her eyes at Jackie. "Start tonight. We can't afford to waste another *minute*."

Sharon was jabbering on the phone to her best friend Linda Taylor when Jackie got home from school. Sharon was home first because Fairfax High classes began an hour earlier than Sidney Lanier's. One day a week Sharon stayed after school for drill team practice and rode the late bus.

The phone was on a little table in the front hall. Since nobody but insurance salesmen ever used the front door, the hall was more like a private alcove. Sharon sprawled on the floor, her feet on the seat of a low-backed chair that went with the table. She cackled at something Linda said.

Jackie sighed. No time like the present to begin

copying Sharon. The things she did to get in Angel Allen's club. A safe distance away, well out of swatting range, she lay down on the floor and put her feet up on the coffee table, parroting Sharon. Pretending to cradle a phone receiver between her jaw and shoulder, she cackled in perfect imitation.

Her unsuspecting role model turned and stared at her. "Hold on a sec," Sharon said to Linda. "Jackie, what are you doing?"

"Nothing."

"You are too doing something. You're bugging me. If you don't get out of here while I'm on the phone — " Sharon kicked her foot to underscore her unspoken threat.

Jackie kicked her foot too. "It's a free country." As long as her sister was occupied on the phone she wasn't worried. The cord only stretched so far.

Sharon's scathing look could have stripped wallpaper. She told Linda she had a kid sister to kill, then hung up. "Why can't I have five minutes privacy! Whatever stupid game you're playing, stop it right now."

"I'm not hurting anything." It felt wonderful to stand up to Sharon, even if she was lying down at the time. "You can't make me leave."

"It's your funeral," Sharon began, but then the phone rang. She pounced on the receiver as if expecting Prince Charles.

"Hel-lo," she breathed in a Marilyn Monroe-type voice.

Jackie eavesdropped openly on the one-way conversation. The caller was obviously a boy. Only a boy could turn her sister into a sweet bunny rabbit. Instead of her usual sharp laughs, Sharon emitted a dainty new laugh, like she was nibbling on a piece of expensive chocolate. Jackie practiced the dainty laugh, wondering how Sharon could keep up that breathy voice without passing out. Her chest felt like she had just had a bad attack of hiccups. After an oozy good-bye Sharon hung up again.

"Who was that?" Jackie cooed.

"Were you here the whole time?" Sharon said in her regular old voice.

"I didn't hear hardly *any*thing, you talked so low. Except the part about meeting after the game Friday," Jackie said, amazed at her sister's ability to switch from bunny to saber-toothed tiger without skipping a beat.

"That's none of your business! And you better not tell Mom, either!" Sharon slammed into her room.

Jackie went into her own room, found an old notebook, and wrote down *When talking to boys, use out-of-breath voice*. She'd have to wait until Sharon came out of her lair before she could record any more of her sister's behavior. Music poured through the heat register in the wall between Sharon's room and Jackie's.

Even without seeing into the next room, Jackie knew Sharon was dancing with her closet door. Sharon loved to put a stack of her favorite records on her stereo, slip into high heels, and dance with her closet door. Her sister looked incredibly dumb swinging around that door, but she *was* one of the best dancers in Fairfax High. She told Jackie often enough. Sharon aspired to audition for *The Milt Grant Show*. Jackie scribbled

Dance with door, though she doubted there would ever be an opportunity to demonstrate this skill in ESG.

Listening to her sister scuffling around the closet door, Jackie suddenly remembered the day they moved into the house, back when she had been a dopey five-year-old. The new house was bigger than their old one in town and Jackie and Sharon could have their own rooms. There wasn't any lawn, yet; scraps of plywood bridged the mud puddles. The woods seemed awfully close. On the back porch, Sharon discovered the dried-up remains of tiny baby black snakes.

Jackie was scared to go to bed that night, all alone in her shadowy room. Then she heard a voice coming from the vent in the wall. "Jack-eee." It was Sharon, speaking to her through the register! From then on, after Jackie was supposed to be in bed, they held whispered converstaions through the heat vent.

They didn't talk through the register any more. Jackie missed hearing her sister's voice drift into her room when the lights were out and she was having trouble getting to sleep. Jackie sighed. Nothing was like it used to be.

During supper, Jackie continued to mirror Sharon's every movement. When Sharon put a pat of butter on her macaroni and cheese, Jackie did the same. When Sharon drank a swallow of iced tea, Jackie drank a sip of iced tea. Sharon cut her pork chop into four pieces, then cut the pieces into smaller bites. Jackie copied. If Sharon had scratched her back with her fork and eaten peas with a knife, Jackie would have, too.

Sharon threw down her napkin. "I can't stand it!"

"Neither can I," Mrs. Howard agreed. "Jackie, why are you mocking Sharon?"

"I'm not mocking her," Jackie said. Well, she wasn't, not really. "I'm just — following her example. You're always telling Sharon to set a good example for me, and now I'm following it."

"Oh, barf! Mom, make her stop. She's just doing it to bug me!" Sharon wadded her paper napkin in a tight ball and hit Jackie with it. Naturally Jackie had to do the same. Sharon slapped Jackie on the arm. Jackie slapped her back.

"Girls!" Mrs. Howard said. "Why do you two always carry on when your father's not here? Jackie, quit mocking Sharon. Nobody likes to be mimicked."

But Jackie didn't know how else to learn to act older. She figured if she imitated Sharon for one whole evening, she would naturally adopt the confident attitude of an almost-senior.

Much of what she was imitating wasn't worth recording, like the way Sharon cut up her pork chop. She did note, however, that Sharon probably never resorted to sticking erasers up her nose during lunch at school, especially if she happened to be sitting next to a boy. With that breathy voice of hers, Sharon would suffocate for sure if she plugged up her nose.

Jackie trailed Sharon into the bathroom with her notebook. Her sister's nightly ritual would definitely be interesting.

"Go away," Sharon said automatically.

"I'm just going to sit right here." Jackie hoisted

herself up on the clothes hamper. "I promise I'll be quiet."

Evidently tired of fighting, Sharon actually allowed her to stay. "I'll be glad when I leave home so I'll have some privacy," she said.

"At least we don't have to share a bedroom any more."

"Thank heavens for that." Sharon smeared Noxema on her forehead. "Sometimes, though, it wasn't too bad. We had some neat pillow fights."

Jackie jotted *Noxema, lots of it* in her notebook, then asked, "Can I put some on?"

Sharon dipped her finger into the jar and wiped a dollop of the white cream on Jackie's cheek.

Jackie was surprised. Sharon was practically treating her like a member of the human race. "Will this make me have nice skin like yours?" Sometimes if she flattered her sister, Sharon acted even nicer.

"I doubt it. You eat too much junk." Sharon examined her eyebrows in the mirror over the sink.

"So do you." Jackie sidled up to the mirror. She could see a portion of her forehead in the corner. "Is that a blackhead?" she screamed, alarmed.

"Where?" Sharon tipped Jackie's chin to the light. She scrubbed at the spot, harder than necessary, Jackie thought. "Just ink. You'll probably get bumps though, any day now. Meanness coming out," she added, quoting their mother. With that famous line, Mrs. Howard often dismissed a mysterious tenth of a degree of fever occurring on test days and miraculously disappearing after the bus had gone.

Concerned, Jackie clambered back up on the clothes hamper, trying to get a better view in the mirror.

"Move out of my light," Sharon said. The nice moment between them, such as it was, was over.

If meanness coming out was going to cause Jackie to have a bad complexion, then Sharon's whole face should have been one big wart.

"Why are you so grumpy?" Jackie asked.

"I don't know." Sharon sighed. "Life, I guess."

"But you have everything! You're pretty and popular and you're on the drill team." Jackie would have given anything to march onto the playing field in a short blue and gray jumper amid cheers, like Sharon did every Friday. "Plus you've had about a zillion boyfriends."

"I don't have one now."

"What's it been — two days since your last date? You could have any guy in the school with a snap of your finger."

Sharon frowned at her reflection. "It's not that easy. You'll find out."

Find out how hard it was to get a guy? Jackie couldn't even get into the club to *talk* about boys, let alone date them. It dawned on her that no crash course would ever teach her to act like a senior, even using her sister as an example. A mature attitude was not something Jackie could pick up by copying.

Bracing her feet against the opposite wall, Jackie balanced the hamper on two knobby casters. "Do you ever wish for the old days?"

"What old days?" Sharon measured the gap between the corner of her eye and her eyebrow with the handle of a toothbrush, the guide she used to see if her eyebrows needed plucking.

Jackie rocked the hamper. "Well, like when we first moved here. Remember the teeny baby snakes we found dead on the back porch?"

"You think of the dumbest stuff. Who cares about that?"

Jackie tried to recall one of the fun times she and her sister had shared. "Remember the time we asked Daddy to go fast over the bump road, and you showed me that trick with peanuts and a Coke?"

The bump road was a country lane that cut through the woods to the Shopping Bag, a little general store. On Sunday afternoons they would often pile in the car and ride to the Shopping Bag where the girls would spend their allowance on Dreamsicles and Clark bars. On the way home, they usually begged their father to speed up as they approached the bump, so they would sail over it and "lose their stomachs," Jackie's term for the weightless feeling they experienced.

On this particular outing Sharon was showing off by dropping salted peanuts in a bottle of Coke. "Don't shake it," Sharon cautioned as she handed the bottle to Jackie. But before Jackie could take a swig, Mr. Howard accelerated and they soared over the bump. Coke foamed out of the bottle like a volcano, fizz and peanuts spewed all over the back seat. Plastered with Coke and syrupy peanuts, they howled with laughter all the way home.

"We lost more than our stomachs that time," Jackie said. "Remember?"

"Not really," Sharon said absently.

"Sure you do. You had Coke all over you . . . the back seat was sticky from then on till Daddy bought the new car." How could Sharon forget such a momentous occasion in their lives?

Suddenly Sharon started giggling.

"What's so funny?"

"I just remembered how we found those gummy peanuts in the crack of the seat and stuffed them in the ashtrays. Whoever cleaned the car out after Dad traded it in must have been surprised."

Jackie laughed. "I forgot that part. The old days were fun, weren't they?"

Sharon said abruptly, "I wish you wouldn't keep bringing up things that happened eons ago. Those days are over and they aren't coming back. Things are different now." She brushed past Jackie's outstretched legs.

Those days certainly were over, Jackie agreed silently. And it was the days ahead she dreaded.

Chapter 4

Natalie greeted Jackie's notes with skepticism. "This isn't going to help us. I mean, who cares if Sharon sprinkles foot powder in her saddle shoes before drill team practice?"

"You would, if you happened to be around her and she didn't," Jackie replied. "Is it no good?"

"Well, the drill team stuff might be useful. If we could learn one of Sharon's routines, we could practice in gym when Angel's around. She'd probably beg us to be in her club. We'd be a definite asset in her group. I mean, look at the way boys drool over cheerleaders. Could you get Sharon to teach us something?"

"You must be kidding. Sharon does everything but wire her drill team rifle with mousetraps. I can't touch it." Slumped over the X-ray Technician folder she was supposed to be studying, Jackie felt leaden with disappointment. She couldn't do anything right, not even copy her own sister. How could Miss Dale expect such a Big Nothing to choose a vocation?

At the beginning of guidance period, Jackie surreptitiously slipped the Forest Ranger folder back into the yellow vocation box, hoping someone had returned Movie Star or Astronaut. The only new job she could find that seemed halfway appealing was X-ray Technician. After skimming the first few paragraphs though, she just couldn't get excited over taking pictures of people's insides.

Natalie was nearly finished with the assignment. Even Angel Allen, sitting on the other side of Jackie, eagerly worked from her Actor/Actress folder. Maybe when Angel was done she'd let Jackie have it next. She might lean across the aisle and say, "We're the only two actress types in here." And the moon was made of green cheese.

"I hope you're not mad at me," Natalie said. "Following Sharon around is still a good idea. How about if I come over to your house one day this week? Maybe we can get her to teach us one of her routines."

When pigs could fly, Jackie thought. But she said, "Okay. Tomorrow?"

Relieved that the role model business wasn't a total loss, Jackie took out the three-page vocation form to work on. The first page had easy questions like name, address, date of birth. Killing time until she could put X-ray Technician back in the yellow box without arousing Miss Dale's suspicions, Jackie filled out the first page in her very best handwriting. She made her letters round and perfectly straight on the line, the way Angel Allen wrote.

Something silky brushed her cheek. Long blond hair. Angel Allen was bending over Jackie's desk, reading her form.

"You were born June second?" Angel blurted. "You just turned twelve! That's just barely past eleven, *mes enfants*!" All seventh-graders were taking French but only Angel used it.

"Well, I — " Jackie stammered, but Angel was already dispensing the news of Jackie's birthdate like a grocer giving away free food.

"Jackie's only been twelve three months!" Marcia Rivett squealed.

Angel said, doodling on the cover of her biology book, "I'll be thirteen next month. I didn't know I was sitting next to a *baby*!"

"Who's a baby? Jackie? Little baby Jackie?" Daryl Forshay began making crying noises. "Ah-wah! Ah-wah-h-h-h!"

Miss Dale squelched the disturbance. "Daryl, we'll have none of that."

Angel, who never seemed to get caught talking in class, whispered a remark to Marcia and they laughed.

Jackie was too mortified to move. Now everybody in the whole room knew she was the youngest. The baby. It wouldn't do any good at all for her and Natalie to pretend they were seniors to impress Angel. As far as Angel was concerned, Jackie might as well be in kindergarten.

"It doesn't matter," Natalie reassured Jackie on the bus the next day. "So what if you had a

38

birthday in June? You're still *twelve*."

"Angel made it sound like I'm still in diapers," Jackie said. At least Natalie was coming home with her to spend the afternoon. Natalie's parents were picking her up after supper, so that gave Natalie and Jackie plenty of time to spy on Sharon.

As soon as they walked in the front door, Jackie noticed two pairs of shoes by the fireplace. "Linda Taylor is here. She's Sharon's best friend."

"Another junior? Great. Now we'll each have a victim to copy."

Jackie's mother brought out a plate of oatmeal cookies. "You girls take what you want, and I'll give the rest to Sharon and Linda."

"We'll bring it to them," Natalie offered. "Save you the trouble." She marched boldly up to Sharon's closed door and walked in without knocking. "Hi, guys. You must be Linda. I'm Natalie."

"That girl doesn't know any strangers," Mrs. Howard said.

Jackie wished she were more like Natalie. Imagine striding into the lion's den like that. Natalie wouldn't have sat like a lump if Angel had teased *her* about her age.

The instant Jackie approached her sister's doorway, Sharon said, right on cue, "Go away. Both of you."

But Natalie set the plate on the bed and began riffling through Sharon's record collection. "Can I play this one? It's my favorite." To Jackie's astonishment, Sharon actually put the album on her stereo.

"When this song is over, you both have to leave," Sharon ordered. But then she and Linda started talking about boys. Jackie and Natalie edged over to the vanity table to play with Sharon's makeup.

"What do you think about Walter Keaton?" Linda asked Sharon, applying lipstick so thickly Jackie wondered why she didn't use a trowel.

"Strictly dogcatcher bait." Sharon daubed silver eyeshadow on the back of her hand to test the color.

"He likes you though."

"His ears stick out like cab doors. And he smells like cabbage." This sent them into peals of laughter. Jackie and Natalie laughed, too.

Sharon frowned at them. "I thought I told you guys to beat it when that song was over."

Natalie leaned over and eased the needle to the beginning of the record. "It's still playing," she said innocently.

Linda brought up another candidate for review. "How about Lennie Smith?"

"Kennel-Ration time."

"I don't think he's so bad," Linda said. "In fact, I kind of like him."

"Lennie Smith?" Sharon was incredulous. "Linda, the guy has a brain the size of a proton."

"I'm not interested in his mind."

"Good thing," Sharon said. "He doesn't have one."

Jackie looked at Natalie. This was exactly the sort of valuable information they needed, how to rate boys. Angel Allen would be impressed to hear them coolly rank the boys in ESG.

Imitating the older girls, Natalie dabbed eyeshadow on the back of her own hand while Jackie outlined her mouth with a bronze lipstick that made her look like one of the faces on Mount Rushmore.

"What do you think of Robert Labson?" Natalie asked Jackie.

"Bow-wow." Jackie barked. "I think he likes you though." The lipstick snapped under the pressure of putting on the third coat. She tried to fit the cap back over the smeary tube.

"I hope not. He wears his jeans too short. And he's got funny feet, haven't you noticed?"

"That's okay," Jackie said. "You're not interested in his feet!" They collapsed in a fit of giggles.

"What is with those two?" Linda asked. "Would you look at what they're doing?"

Sharon exploded. "I told you kids to get lost. Jackie Howard, you broke my best lipstick!" She grabbed her wooden drill-team rifle and swung it at them.

The girls fled to Jackie's room.

"Whew, that was close," Jackie panted. "Sharon must be slipping. She could have clobbered us."

"Probably because I'm company. Still, we learned some really good stuff." Natalie got up and wandered around the room. She had been to Jackie's house only once before, when they were first becoming friends.

"My room is bigger than yours," Natalie observed. "But it's got this ugly green carpet. And the kid who had the room before me painted the walls blue with a white stripe across one wall."

"Sounds neat." Jackie could just imagine her

41

mother letting her paint a white stripe across the wall.

"It isn't. I'd rather have plain pink walls like yours." Natalie stopped to read Jackie's birth certificate, framed and hanging over her bed. "How come you have this? So people will know you weren't hatched?"

Jackie giggled. "Mama framed both our birth certificates. Sharon took hers down." The document had a photograph of the Columbia Hospital for Women, where Jackie and Sharon were born, and Jackie's tiny hand- and footprints.

"I bet your mom hated cleaning all that black gunk off you. Hey! You were born in Washington, D.C."

"District of Columbia," Jackie corrected. She always felt strange to have been born in the United States, but not in any state. Her birthdate was written in curliqued letters on the certificate. She hoped Natalie wouldn't make a big deal out of it, the way Angel had. It was bad enough being the youngest in the class.

The stereo went silent next door. Without the blast of music, they could hear wavering voices.

"Where's that coming from?" Natalie asked.

"Here." Jackie knelt down by the heat vent.

Natalie put her ear over the grill. "You can hear everything they're saying."

"I know. It's better than an intercom."

Sharon's voice wafted up through the aluminum register. "Do you think Mickey Rowe is cute?"

Linda's reply was muffled.

Sharon must have been standing right beside the grill because every syllable was distinct. "I kind of like him," she confided. "I just love those greenish-blue eyes of his . . . he's kind of serious, though."

"A bookworm." That was Linda's opinion.

"Not really. I've seen him looking at me in English." Sharon's next comments were garbled. Then she moved back to the heat vent again. " — need to find out how much he likes me. I'll ask him to the Halloween party . . . be plenty of chances . . ."

"What Halloween party?" Jackie said. This was a news flash to her.

Natalie shrugged. "You live here. I don't."

Just then Mrs. Howard came in to let the girls know supper was nearly ready. "What are you doing huddled around the heat vent? Are you cold?"

Jackie jumped up. "Is Sharon having a Halloween party here?"

"I'm afraid so. She asked me last week if she could have a small party in the basement, and like a fool I said yes."

Jackie clutched Natalie's arm. "Do you know what this means? Now I can tell Angel that we're having a Halloween party with *older* kids! Then she'll be sorry she made fun of me today."

Natalie could barely contain her excitement. "She'll probably ask you to be in her club, and you can tell her you won't join without me!"

"I hate to put a damper on your plans," Mrs. Howard broke in. "But Sharon is only inviting kids from her class."

"Surely she'll let me and Natalie come. We don't take up much room. And we won't eat a thing. We won't touch the food, will we, Natalie?" Natalie shook her head solemnly.

"I'm sorry, girls, but I think Sharon is pretty set on having things her way."

"She always has everything her way!" Jackie protested. "A Halloween party right in my house and I can't go!"

"Now, Jackie," her mother soothed. "You wouldn't want Sharon horning in on your party, would you? Listen, we'll have our own little party upstairs. Just you and Daddy and me. And Natalie. You come, too. It'll be fun." She left to tend to supper.

Jackie stubbed the toe of her shoe into the rug. "It'll be fun, all right. About as much fun as going to the dentist."

Ever optimistic, Natalie said, "Maybe Sharon will change her mind and let us come."

"And maybe tomorrow I'll wake up rich and famous. You don't have an older sister. You have no idea how awful they are."

"I've got three little brothers. They're awful enough." Natalie shook a miniature glass bottle with a shiny copper penny inside, one of Sharon's souvenirs from her long-ago field trip to Williamsburg. Jackie had been so fascinated with the penny in the bottle that Sharon finally gave it to her. "We can still play this party angle to get in Angel's club."

"Are you deaf? I just said Sharon would never change her mind in a million years — "

Natalie waved her away. "Not about going to the party. We can talk it up in front of Angel. You know, like it's our party and only older kids are invited. That'll make her notice us."

"She's already noticed me," Jackie said

44

glumly. "And not the way I want, either."

"She'll forget all about what happened today when she hears we're running with an older crowd."

Jackie wasn't so certain. "I think we need to do something really dramatic to get in Angel's club."

"Like what?"

"I don't know." How could she think of something dramatic to do when she wasn't even able to come up with a vocation topic for her guidance report?

"Don't worry," Natalie said. "You'll get a brilliant idea. Meanwhile, let's play up Sharon's party."

But a week before the party, Sharon fell through the living room ceiling in a friend's house, upstaging whatever dramatic act Jackie was considering.

Chapter 5

"Left face march." Jackie stepped smartly to the left. She pretended to wait until an imaginary regiment turned, column by column, before snapping her body into the required position. Her rake was too big to twirl like Sharon's drill team rifle, but it would have been suicide to borrow the rifle even though Sharon wasn't home.

"Jackie!" her mother called. "Let's get busy."

Reluctantly, Jackie made a half-hearted pass around the clothesline poles. It was one of those wonderful crisp fall Saturdays that made a person glad to be alive. Glad, that is, until her mother insisted the backyard had to be raked or else. Sharon was supposed to be helping. But she and Linda Taylor had gone to another friend's house to practice drill team routines.

Jackie pushed leaves into a pile. Why did they have such a big yard? The woods produced enor-

mous quantities of leaves, which were pretty —
on the trees. Jackie admired them as much as
the next person. Purple sweet gum, scarlet dog-
wood, yellow poplar, and especially the oak, a
color that could not be described or duplicated.
When she made paper leaves in the third grade,
she'd use six or seven crayons on her oak leaf,
layered one on top of the other, and never come
near the true shade. But now the leaves were a
pain and her parents' obsession with keeping
the place like a putting green was ridiculous.

She pictured Sharon marching in her short-
skirted uniform, like she was leading a parade
down Constitution Avenue, and felt the acidy
beginnings of envy in her stomach. How did
Sharon manage to get out of her share of work
time and again? It was same way Angel Allen
never got caught talking in class. People must
be born like that, she concluded. When Sharon
was a little baby, she probably yanked the cat's
tail and dumped her oatmeal on the floor and
everybody just said, "Isn't she cute?" When
Jackie came along, she couldn't holler even if
she was being stabbed with a diaper pin. It
wasn't fair. Sharon got everything. A Halloween
party, no work, and the glory of marching in the
drill team. All Jackie had was a pile of leaves
and a blister.

"How much more?" Jackie asked her mother,
who was working on the other side of the yard.

"Finish that corner and then we can take a
break."

That "corner" was the size of a football field.
She was surprised her mother didn't make her
rake the woods just to neaten things up. Jackie

was almost done when a black missile streaked out from under the porch and dive-bombed into the pile, flinging leaves everywhere.

"Felix! Look what Sharon's cat did!"

Her mother laughed. "He's just playing."

Sharon's cat was just another reminder of how unfair life was. Four years ago, the girls were each allowed to choose a kitten from a litter a neighbor was giving away. Sharon selected the only black kitten, a devilish imp she named Felix. Jackie picked a sweet gray female with a pinkish spot on her nose.

Jackie played dress-up with her cat, draping the cat's body with her mother's beads. Sometimes, when no one was around, Jackie would let her cat eat off her own plate. One rainy April day her cat ran away. Jackie searched the cold, dripping woods the whole evening but never found a trace of her beloved cat.

Mrs. Howard told the girls that Felix now belonged to them both, but Jackie didn't want anything to do with Sharon's little monster. Once she wrapped a strand of crystal beads around Felix's ears and he bit her. Sharon's cat was just like Sharon, mean and hateful.

"I don't know why I have to work while Sharon has all the fun," Jackie grumbled, digging up clumps of grass as well as leaves with the tines of her rake.

"Sharon's helping me with the front yard tomorrow," Mrs. Howard said. "She'll work plenty. The front yard is all downhill, you know."

Though they were several yards from the house, Jackie heard the phone ringing. "Phone!"

48

she yelled, flying indoors. Any diversion from work was welcome, even somebody trying sell them a magazine subscription.

The woman on the other end sounded upset as she asked to speak to Jackie's mother. Jackie ran back outside "Mom! It's the lady where Sharon went visiting."

"What does she want?" Mrs. Howard wondered as she propped her rake against the porch. "If Sharon thinks she can spend the night at that girl's house. . . ."

Jackie loitered in the hall and listened to her mother's responses. It seemed to be bad news about Sharon.

When she hung up, Mrs. Howard said, "The Cross's are bringing Sharon home. They were calling from the emergency room, at the hospital. Sharon and some others were fooling around in the attic and Sharon fell through the living room ceiling! She's okay, but her ribs are scraped pretty bad."

"How'd she do that?" Jackie asked. Sharon was in real trouble, all right, she thought with a little flip of joy. But even as she gloated, she worried whether her sister was hurt more seriously.

"They were up in the attic, where they weren't supposed to be, and Sharon stepped off a joist. The attic must be like ours, without a finished floor."

Jackie nodded, imagining the scene. She was only allowed up in their attic at Christmastime, to help bring the decorations down. Exposed joists padded with insulation made their attic treacherous as a tiger pit. One false step and you'd break through the plaster. Which was apparently what Sharon did.

Her mother checked the window, even though it was too soon to expect Sharon home. "I don't even know these people! How could Sharon fall through the living room ceiling in some strange house?"

Jackie couldn't quite see the logic of that. "Would you want Sharon to fall through *our* attic? Then we'd have the big hole in *our* ceiling."

A short while later, a car pulled into their driveway. Sharon and a woman got out. The woman spoke to Mrs. Howard outside, but Sharon walked stiffly into the house. Except for a few iodine-painted scratches on her arms, she didn't look any different to Jackie, who was anticipating her sister to be bound up like a mummy.

"Boy, are you in for it," Jackie said.

Sharon flung her purse in a chair.

"You don't seem very hurt to me."

"A fat lot you know." Sharon lifted the edge of her blouse. Under a wide gauze bandage, iodine seeped through like blood. She sucked in her bottom lip as she eased her blouse back into the waistband of her skirt. Jackie figured it must hurt like anything just to move.

Outside, the car engine started up again. Jackie went to the window. "Those people are leaving. Here comes Mama. What are you going to do?" When Jackie was in trouble, the doomsday feeling that descended while waiting to confront her mother was worse than any punishment.

"What can I do?" But her voice trembled.

Sharon put up a brave front but inwardly she was scared.

"Let me see," Mrs. Howard said when she came back in. Sharon dutifully lifted her blouse again, wincing a lot more than she did the first time, Jackie thought. Mrs. Howard sighed. "What happened?"

"Janet's mother must have told you. What else were you two talking about out there all that time? The weather?"

"Don't sass me, Sharon. I want to hear what happened in your own words."

"You won't believe me," Sharon said defensively. "It's always my word against somebody else's." Jackie was amazed. Even with scraped ribs and facing a possible sentence of being grounded the rest of the century, Sharon had the nerve to talk back.

What was left of Mrs. Howard's patience was unraveled. "What were you doing up in the attic when you knew you weren't supposed to be there?"

"We were looking for an old yearbook of Janet's. Her brother followed us up there, him and these friends of his. One of them pushed me off a rafter and I fell through. It wasn't my fault!"

"Where was Janet's mother?"

"Next door," Sharon said. "I was lying on the couch and then Linda's leg came through the ceiling beside my hole just as Mrs. Cross came in. She took one look and started to cry."

"I'm not surprised," Mrs. Howard said sourly. "Do you have idea how much it will cost to repair their ceiling?"

"Probably a fortune," Jackie put in.

Sharon didn't even glance at her. "Shut up, twerp."

Mrs. Howard said, "Jackie, keep out of this. Sharon, the Cross's are being very nice about it. They felt bad a child was hurt in their house. They said we wouldn't have to pay for the ceiling, but of course we want to, just as they paid for your doctor bill."

"So take it out of that pittance of an allowance you give me," Sharon said, standing up. "Can I go to my room now? I really don't feel so hot."

Sharon didn't come out for supper. Jackie ate with her parents, listening to them discuss Sharon.

"She's always been the rebellious one," Mrs. Howard said to her husband, apparently forgetting Jackie was there. "Remember that business about Sunday school?"

Jackie remembered. When Sharon was eleven, she declared she no longer wanted to attend Sunday school. "I go to school five days a week," she had argued. "Why should I have to go on Sunday, too? All we do in there is play hangman."

Her parents were stunned at this outburst, but then Mr. Howard had said, "She's old enough to make up her own mind. If she doesn't want to go, it won't do any good to send her."

Jackie, who was seven at the time, began to cry. Sharon turned to her. "What are you blubbering about?"

"Because," Jackie sobbed. "If you don't go to Sunday school, neither can I and I won't get my wreath!"

Sharon blew up like a firecracker. "Is that the

only reason I should go to Sunday school? So Jackie can get a dumb wreath? It's not fair."

Mr. Howard solved the problem by taking Jackie to Sunday school himself. Sharon stayed home and read the funnies. When Jackie proudly displayed her wreath-encircled pin, which signified two years of perfect attendance, Sharon remarked, "Good for you," nice as pie. Of course, Sharon could afford to be nice. She had what she wanted, freedom on Sundays, while all Jackie had was an enameled pin.

"Sharon's headstrong," Mr. Howard said now. "She always has been, and she always will be. This isn't a phase she's going through. It's the way Sharon is."

Her mother put soup and a sandwich on a tray. "Jackie, take this in to your sister."

"She won't let me in her room."

"Well, go in anyway. She needs to eat, and your father and I need to talk."

Sharon was lying down when Jackie went in. "I'll never be able to sleep. Or do my drill team routines. And I've got a game Friday."

"Mama said you should eat this." Jackie set the tray on the floor. Felix jumped off the bed and immediately began to investigate. She shooed him away. "It's good. Cream of tomato, just the way you like it."

Sharon got up stiffly, as if she had a board taped to her back. "What are they doing out there, talking about me?"

Jackie nodded. "Daddy said you're headstrong. You always were, and you always will be."

Sharon groaned. "Good grief. What did Mom say?"

"She told me to give you this because they needed to talk without me around."

"They're probably torn between locking me in my room for life or sending me to Ivacota Farm." Ivacota Farm was a legendary correctional institute for wayward girls back in the fifties. Although the farm no longer existed, Mrs. Howard often held it out as the ultimate threat if the girls didn't shape up.

"Did it hurt when you fell through the ceiling?" Jackie asked.

Sharon nibbled at half the sandwich. "It didn't tickle. The fall wasn't so bad because it wasn't that far, and it happened so fast. But the plaster was jagged around the hole and it just about ripped me to pieces."

"How long do you have to wear that bandage?"

Sharon shrugged. "Tills it heals, I guess. The doctor said I was lucky I didn't crack a rib."

Mrs. Howard came in, closing the door behind her. "How are you feeling?"

"So-so." Sharon waggled her hand back and forth. "Trying to sleep tonight ought to be a barrel of laughs."

"You'll have to sleep on your back," Mrs. Howard said. "Is that all you're going to eat?"

"I'm not hungry." Sharon crawled into bed again. Jackie noticed her sister's injuries always seemed worse when their mother was around.

"She's worried about what you and Daddy are going to do to her," said Jackie.

"That's what I want to talk to you about," Mrs. Howard told Sharon.

Sharon turned her head to the wall. "Go ahead. Lower the boom."

"Sharon, you did this to yourself, so don't blame me. Your father and I decided to have you excused from the game this week — "

"I knew it!" Sharon shrieked.

"I'm making an appointment for you with our doctor on Friday, and if he says you're well enough to march the following week, then you can. Plus you're grounded for the week."

"Is that all? Why don't you give me forty lashes, too?" Sharon's voice was muffled by her pillow.

Jackie knew her sister was really miserable about missing the game. "Look at it this way, Sharon, at least they didn't cancel your party Saturday night."

Sharon glared at Jackie. "Don't bring that up! Now Mom and Dad *will* call it off!"

"We're not calling off the party," Mrs. Howard said. "Though we almost did. But you're on probation, Sharon. If you do anything else . . ." She didn't have to finish the sentence.

When their mother left, Sharon hurled her pillow at Jackie. "You practically got my party canceled!"

"Better not hit me or I'll tell. Remember what Mama said."

"If you do anything to wreck my party, you're going to be sorry."

Jackie slammed the door with satisfaction. For once she had the upper hand! Without her cooperation, Sharon's party was down the drain. If Sharon had been home raking leaves like she was supposed to, instead of goofing off, she wouldn't be in this fix. Then Jackie remembered Sharon's half of the yard had yet to be raked. Sharon was certainly in no condition to work. Guess who would have to do it for her? The entire front yard, all downhill!

Chapter 6

The closer it got to Saturday night, the faster
Sharon's scraped ribs healed. Jackie was sure her
sister's miraculous recovery would make medical
history. When Sharon went to the store to buy
decorations for her party, her ribs hardly hurt at
all, but if their mother asked her to wipe a dish,
suddenly Sharon could barely move.

In homeroom, Jackie and Natalie planned their
strategy. They would discuss the Halloween
party, loud enough for Angel to overhear, making it sound as though the older kids wouldn't
even *have* the party without Jackie and Natalie.

"We'll do it during the break between English
and social studies," Natalie instructed. "I'll ask
you about the party, and you take it from there.
Make sure Angel is listening. And lay it on
thick."

Jackie could hardly wait for the English section
of ESG to be over. At last Miss Dale called the

break and the class exploded from its usual stupor to hyperactivity. Kids raced to the front to sharpen pencils or line up for the pass to the rest rooms.

Natalie yawned nonchalantly, the image of someone wavering between attending a polo match or a jaunt on a yacht.

"Hey, Jackie," she said, super-casually and a little too loud. "How're the plans for the party coming along? Does Lennie Smith still want you to dance every single dance with him?"

"Definitely," Jackie replied, flipping her hand in an I-couldn't-care-less gesture. "But I told him Pete Dial asked me first. He's captain of the football team." Pete Dial, the only name that flitted into her head, was actually the man who repaired their lawn mower.

"Captain of the Fairfax Rebels," she repeated, enunciating each syllable for Angel's benefit. "A *senior* at Fairfax High. Of course, everybody there will be a *junior* or *senior*."

"What a blast we're going to have! Dancing with older guys the whole night! And Lennie Smith is no slouch. He's captain of the *basketball* team at Fairfax High. Imagine having two captains fight over you!" Natalie batted her eyelashes at the wonder of it all.

"The captain of the track team said he was dying to meet you," Jackie said and then she wished she hadn't. With that many captains under one roof, the Halloween party was starting to sound more like a Joint Chiefs of Staff meeting at the Pentagon. She shifted in her seat to see if Angel was taking it all in.

Angel pulled a tissue from a purse-pack and

blew her nose. She had blown her nose a lot during English. If she was impressed by the fabulous Halloween party plans, she gave no indication.

"He told me so himself," Jackie continued, afraid to speak any louder without attracting unwanted attention from Daryl Forshay.

"Who told you what himself?" Natalie opened her English book and stood it up on her desk, making a crude sound deflector.

"The captain of the track team! About meeting you at Shar — I mean, *our* party. He told me yesterday when we went to Gifford's to pick up the cake." Angel's indifference was rattling her.

Natalie shook her head. Jackie had blundered somehow — the cake! Nobody would pick up a cake for a party so far in advance.

"It's a special cake," she improvised. "It doesn't get stale — it's got this new kind of icing. And because it was so big, they couldn't bake it at the last minute. So we picked it up yesterday, the captain of the track team and me. It has to feed fifty people!"

Now Natalie was waving her arms. Jackie was making a bad situation even worse. Too much detail about the stupid cake. Get back to the important part, the *boys*.

Angel blew her nose again. Break was almost over. Flustered, Jackie couldn't think of anything else to say.

Natalie rushed to the rescue. "How many boys did you invite?"

"Forty." A good round number.

"Not too many girls, I hope." Natalie was straining to keep the dialogue going.

Jackie remembered she had said the cake would feed fifty. "Only ten. You and me and my sister, who's a *junior*. Plus Sharon's girlfriends. But they're all ugly," she added hastily, so Angel wouldn't think the older girls presented any competition.

"Forty boys and ten girls!" Natalie said. "Great ratio."

Miss Dale closed the door and began the social studies lesson. Jackie glanced sidelong at Angel. The girl had not shown a flicker of interest. Even Susan Ryan, who sat behind Natalie, had drooled over every word. Jackie was just about convinced that nothing short of a fancy-dress ball at Buckingham Palace would capture Angel's attention, when Miss Dale called on Angel to answer a question from the night before's homework.

"Angel," said Miss Dale. "Did you hear me?"

Marcia Rivett nudged Angel. "Teacher's talking to you."

"Pardon? Did you ask me something, Miss Dale?" Angel blew her nose again. "I have this terrible cold, and my ears are all stuffed."

Jackie pinched back a scream of anguish. Angel's ears were stuffed! The whole conversation was a complete, total waste because she'd never *heard* any of it.

Sharon spent a lot of time on the phone with Linda, making last-minute arrangements for Saturday. Jackie chafed at being excluded from the plans.

"Sharon won't let me do anything," she griped to her mother the day of the big event.

"It's her party," Mrs. Howard said mildly.

"But it's not fair! I've been good all week. Why can't I help some?"

"Have you asked her?"

"Ask the Queen of the Universe? Can't you *make* her let me help?" It was a last resort, but it usually worked.

Her mother called Sharon out to the kitchen. When Sharon arrived, Mrs. Howard said, "Jackie wants to help you get ready for the party."

Sharon glanced at Jackie. "Has the baby been whining again? I don't need her help. Linda's coming over early to help me."

"Linda will be here half the night as it is," Mrs. Howard pointed out. "She doesn't have to be here all day, too. Call her back and tell her not to come early. It won't kill you to let Jackie help. Your sister's a good worker."

"She's a pest. She'll ruin everything! But naturally Mama's precious baby has to have her way!"

"I do not!" Jackie protested.

"You do, too. You always get everything just because you're the youngest." Sharon stalked off to phone Linda.

The next afternoon, Sharon stonily handed Jackie the push broom. "Sweep the whole basement," she commanded. "That means the corners and behind the furnace. When you're done with that, hose the floor down."

"What're you going to do?" Jackie wanted to know.

"Just sweep and mind your own business."

The basement smelled musty, like a sack of old potatoes stored under the sink too long.

61

Sharon cranked open the small, high-up windows. Immediately an autumn-spiced breeze wafted in. Jackie reflected on all the past Halloween nights she had gone trick-or-treating with her cousins in Manassas. She wished she could go back to being eleven again, just for tonight. Either that or old enough to attend Sharon's party. Being in-between was such a drag.

With another broom, Sharon knocked down cobwebs.

"You ought to leave a couple," Jackie suggested. "So it'll look spookier."

Sharon didn't say a word, but Jackie noticed Sharon left a few spider webs.

Sweeping the whole basement, and then hosing it down and sweeping excess water into the drain, took Jackie almost an hour and rewarded her with dime-sized callouses. "Now what?" she asked her sister, hoping for a less grueling task like hanging crepe paper.

"Set the folding chairs up by the freezer," Sharon said.

The old metal chairs they used for reunions and picnics had been left out in the rain so many times nothing short of dynamite would make them unfold. Jackie mashed her fingers time and time again, but she finally managed to line up a neat row of chairs. "How's this?"

Sharon frowned. "It looks like a recital, not a party."

Jackie rearranged the chairs, wondering why anyone would bother to come to Grouch-Box's party.

"Now scrub the table with Ajax," Sharon ordered next.

"But aren't you going to use that plastic tablecloth you bought?" Jackie couldn't see the sense in washing a table that would be covered up.

"Just do like I tell you."

Jackie scrubbed the old chrome dinette table until her knuckles were raw. Sharon sat on the bottom step and punched out cardboard witches and bats from a decorations book she had bought. It didn't require the IQ of Einstein to figure out that Sharon was purposely giving her the dirty jobs. If this was a costume party, Jackie could come as a pound of ground meat.

"Now what, Master? Want me to asphalt the driveway? Trim the front yard with manicure scissors?"

"I guess we've done enough cleaning." Sharon surveyed the basement. "But it's still so depressing down here. I wish we had a rec room, like Linda has in her house. It looks terrible! We can't have a party here!"

"Halloween parties are supposed to be creepy," Jackie remarked. "Put a sign outside that says This Way to the Dungeon, and people won't expect much."

Sharon's glance told her what she thought of that. "The lights are so harsh. It's like being grilled in a police station." She was right. The naked bulbs illuminated part of the basement too sharply, leaving the corners in gloomy shadow.

"I can make shades to put over the lights. It'll look really cool, Sharon. You'll see." She scampered upstairs and ran back down again with a package of construction paper and Scotch tape.

Working quickly, she fashioned an orange paper lampshade. When she held it over the bare light bulb, the effect was softer, more mysterious.

"Hey, that's great!" Sharon said, pleased. Then she broke down and let Jackie tape witch and black cat cutouts to the cinder block walls.

"How are you girls doing?" Mrs. Howard asked, coming down the steps with a bundle of corn shocks. "Well! I hardly recognize the place!"

"Did Daddy save me those when he cut the corn? Isn't he sweet?" Sharon propped the corn shock in the corner next to the table. "It's perfect!"

"Not quite." Mr. Howard carried down a huge carved jack o'lantern and set it on the table. "Now it's perfect." Then he spotted the paper lampshades. "Who did that?"

"Jackie," Sharon said, giving her sister credit for the first time since she was born. "It was her idea."

Sharon was so delighted with the transformed room, and the fact that her party would start in another two hours, she actually invited Jackie to help her bring down the record player. Happiness, Jackie concluded as she lugged a huge stack of albums down the stairs, made her sister positively giddy. Too bad Sharon couldn't have a party every day.

"Isn't it time for you to get ready?" Jackie asked, hoping Sharon's generosity would extend to letting Jackie and Natalie stay for the festivities. "It's almost six."

"In a minute." Sharon twirled, hugging herself. In her exuberance she even hugged Jackie.

"Isn't it exciting! I love Halloween! I think it's my favorite holiday in the whole year."

"More than Christmas?"

"More than my birthday!" Pulling a bottle of nail polish from her pocket, Sharon began writing something on an empty thumbtack card. "Want to know something?"

"What?"

"It's sort of a secret."

Her sister must be delirious to divulge a secret! "Are you sure you want to tell me?"

Sharon's lips curved in a smile Jackie had never seen before. "The only reason I'm having this party is to find out if a certain boy likes me."

Of course Jackie and Natalie had heard Sharon confiding to Linda the day they listened through the heat vent. She had to act surprised, though. Arching her eyebrows up to her hairline, Jackie said, "Really and truly? Who's the boy?"

Sharon capped the nail polish bottle and flourished the card. "Him."

" 'Mick Rowe,' " Jackie read. "Who's he?"

"Just about the cutest guy at Fairfax. He's a little shy, which is why I decided to have this party." Pacing the length of the basement, she continued, "After we eat, I'm going to play slower music and ask him to dance. We'll dance over to here." She pointed to the furnace. "Then Linda is supposed to cut the lights off. Before the lights come back on, I'll know whether Mick likes me as much as I think he does."

Sharon left to get dressed. Jackie strolled around, wishing the story she and Natalie had made up for Angel's benefit were true — that forty boys, all captains of some team or another, were fighting to dance with her. Would she ever be old enough to dance with a boy and hear him say he liked her? She doubted it. She didn't even know how to dance, much less maneuver a boy over to the furnace in the dark. Boys were a mystery, like the penny in the bottle or the color of oak leaves in the fall. Sharon excelled in the subject of boys, but of course, she was Somebody.

Jackie went upstairs to help her mother with the refreshments.

Chapter 7

Jackie's hopes of being allowed to stay for Sharon's party died when Sharon came out of her room, wearing a new skirt and sweater and her old familiar scowl.

"How come you're right by the door where everyone can see you?" she asked suspiciously. "Stay out of sight."

"What do you want me to do? Lock myself in a closet?" Jackie had set the plastic pumpkin she used for trick or treat last year on the end table and was unsuccessfully posing Felix by it so the guests would have a real Halloween shock when they came in. The cat absolutely refused to cooperate. His claws slashed her arm as he dashed to freedom. "Ouch!" she cried.

"Don't aggravate him, and he won't scratch you." Sharon checked her appearance in the oval mirror. "And lose that tacky pumpkin. I already have a real jack o'lantern."

Jackie stuffed the plastic pumpkin behind the sofa. The closeness they had shared in the basement was gone. Sharon was in her grown-up world, relegating Jackie back to the sandbox. Would they ever be in the same world together, at the same time?

Sharon sailed into the kitchen. "Mom, is the food ready yet? People are going to *be* here soon, and I don't want you or Dad traipsing downstairs after the party starts."

Jackie followed her sister into the kitchen. Mrs. Howard garnished a tray of "goblin canapes," Jackie's creation, crustless peanut butter and grape jelly sandwiches with faces cut out of the top slices of bread so the purple jelly oozed through.

"Are you sure peanut butter and jelly isn't too babyish?" Sharon asked.

"You still eat peanut butter, don't you? I thought we decided it was too damp in the basement for hot food like hamburgers," Mrs. Howard replied.

"I know, but I don't want people to think we're *cheap*, serving peanut butter."

"Not the way Jackie did those little faces. They look catered."

But Sharon had already moved on to her next anxiety. "What about the sour-cream dip? And the dessert?"

"Both ready. You can take them down. Get the dip out of the refrigerator."

Sharon stepped back, tripping over Jackie. "What's *she* doing in the way? Being a pest as usual."

"If you ask me," Jackie said to no one in particular, "the dip isn't in the refrigerator."

"Mom! Make her go to her room!"

"Jackie's not hurting anything. You can't carry all this food by yourself."

Sharon snatched the chilled silver dish and a huge bag of chips and went downstairs.

"She's just nervous," her mother said, handing Jackie the platter of orange-iced brownies.

"I'm surprised she doesn't have me deported to Devil's Island," Jackie remarked. It had been *her* idea to drizzle melted chocolate over the icing in a spider's web design, but did Sharon thank her? Nooo. Sharon was glad enough for Jackie's slave labor when the basement was hopelessly filthy. But now that things were exactly the way Sharon wanted them, she couldn't stand to be in the same time zone with her sister.

Downstairs, the candlelit jack o'lantern eerily grinned, and Jackie's paper shades filtered just enough light to give the party atmosphere. Jackie set the brownie platter on one end of the table and snitched an M&M from a bowl.

"Out of the food!" Sharon yelled.

"I only took one rotten M&M. I'm sure you won't miss it. Besides, it was a brown one."

"Upstairs, right now."

"I think I just heard the doorbell," Jackie said.

Sharon practically bulldozed Jackie in her haste to answer the door first. Linda Taylor and a tall boy with glasses stood on the porch.

"Hi! You all go downstairs," Sharon greeted her guests. "There are Cokes and stuff to eat."

Jackie escorted them to the basement entrance.

"I had a pumpkin here so you'd know where it was, but Sharon told me it looked tacky. I'm Jackie," she said to Linda's date.

"Sharon's little sister." Linda spoke to the boy as if Jackie were an inanimate object.

The boy had better manners. "Hello, Jackie-Sharon's-little-sister. Are you coming to the party, too?"

"Are you kidding? Sharon would kill me." Then she remembered the day Sharon and Linda ranked boys. "Hey, you must be the one with the brain the size of a pro — "

"JACKIE!" Sharon grabbed the back of her neck in a hammerlock. "Somebody let her out of her cage."

Lennie ruffled Jackie's hair. "I think your kid sister is cute."

Jackie's heart swelled with instant adoration. A junior boy actually thought she was cute! "Your brain is a whole lot bigger than a proton," she said generously.

Sharon pushed her friends toward the basement, flashing Jackie a look of pure contempt. "You and your smart mouth! Go to your room."

Jackie stood her ground. "I'm waiting for Natalie. I have a perfect right to sit here by the door and wait for my friend."

The doorbell ding-donged again. Natalie entered with a bunch of Sharon's friends. "Isn't this neat? All these guys!"

"Mo-ther!" Sharon called. "Will you come get the *children*?"

Mrs. Howard herded the girls into the kitchen. "We'll have our own little party out here. See the brownies Jackie made?"

"Those are the ones that didn't turn out. We're eating Sharon's old leftovers," Jackie said dismally. A party in the kitchen with her parents was hardly her idea of a rousing good time, especially when there was at least one boy downstairs who thought she was cute.

"They still taste good." Her father put down the newspaper and sampled a goblin sandwich with a messed-up face. "Mmmmm. My favorite."

Natalie punched Jackie. Jackie giggled. For some reason, things were funnier when Natalie was around.

The basement door slammed for the last time. Music blasted from below. Sharon's party was in full swing.

"Where are all your trick or treaters?" Natalie asked. "When I left my place, there was a big gang of them coming down our street."

"We don't have any," Jackie said. "Nobody ever comes way out here."

"You mean you've never been trick or treating?" Natalie was saucer-eyed with disbelief.

"Of course I have." Jackie felt a prickle of irritation. Why did people think because they didn't live in the suburbs they milked cows and rode mules?

"We drove the girls to Manassas and let them go around with their cousins," Mrs. Howard explained. "When Jackie was too little to go trick or treating with Sharon, I'd let her hand the candy out. This was when we lived in town. She'd always scream when she saw the kids in their costumes, scared to death. And then when I took her around the first time — I guess she was four — she wouldn't go up to the door and let people give her candy!"

Jackie wanted to slither under the table. How dare her mother dredge up embarrassing stories in front of Natalie? It was bad enough they were barred from the party and forced to eat rejected sandwiches, without having to listen to what a big baby Jackie had been.

"Let's go outside," Jackie said to Natalie. "We can spy on Sharon's party from out there."

The night was clear and crisp, perfect for Halloween. A three-quarter moon hung crookedly in the sky, like one of the decorations Jackie had taped to the walls. A light breeze rustled dead leaves hanging from skeletal branches.

"It's *dark* out here," Natalie whispered. "Didn't you bring a flashlight?"

"For what? Besides, somebody down there might see us if we flashed a light all over the place." Jackie stooped to peer into the ground-level basement window. A few kids were dancing. Most of them crowded around the refreshment table, shouting to be heard over the stereo. "Boy, are they having fun."

But Natalie wasn't even looking in at the party. She stared at the woods, a solid black outline against the ink-washed sky. "Is that the nearest house, that one way over there?"

"Yeah. The Martins, these old people."

"You don't have any streetlights, either." Natalie's voice sounded shaky and distant.

Jackie rubbed the glass to see better. "What do we need streetlights for? I know where everything is." She knelt closer to the window. "I wonder if that's Mick Rowe over there with Sharon. He's the one she likes."

Natalie stood up suddenly. "I'm cold. Let's go back in the house."

"But it's not — " Then Jackie realized her friend was scared of the dark, menacing woods. Natalie was used to living in developments where only a few tame trees were planted to look pretty.

"I'm cold, too," Jackie said, even though she really wasn't. "Anyway, we can't see that good from here."

The party in the kitchen had fizzled. Mr. Howard had retired to the living room. Mrs. Howard hauled six-packs of soft drinks from the laundry porch. "They ran out of sodas already. Would you girls take these down?"

Jackie glanced joyfully at Natalie. They had a legitimate reason to crash Sharon's party!

"Watch the stairs now," Mrs. Howard cautioned. Jackie would have gladly slid down the steps in a toboggan.

The basement was jammed with teenagers. Jackie never realized her sister had so many friends. Hands reached for the drinks before she and Natalie ever made it to the refreshment table.

"Here they are!" a red-haired boy cried over the deafening racket of music and laughter. "Our loyal St. Bernards! You're supposed to go 'woof,' " he coached Jackie.

She giggled. Sharon's friends were funny! If only she and Natalie could stay without Sharon finding out. Jackie spotted her sister over by the furnace, talking to a boy in a blue shirt. She seemed very engrossed. Maybe if they kept a low profile, Sharon would never know they were there.

Jackie led Natalie to the refreshment table. After splitting the remaining soft drinks, they helped themselves to sandwiches without messed-up faces and brownies with all the corners intact. The party food tasted so much better than the leftovers they had eaten upstairs.

It wasn't long before Sharon saw them. She hustled right over, bristling with annoyance. "What are you two doing down here?"

"We brought down the rest of the drinks," Jackie replied. "Mama told us. So there."

"Well, you can march back *up*stairs." Sharon propelled Jackie in the direction of the steps.

"Let us stay!" Jackie pleaded. "We won't bother anything. We'll sit right by the stereo and change records for you, won't we, Natalie?"

"We promise not to cause trouble." Natalie said.

The red-haired boy intercepted them. "Aw, let the kids stay, Sharon. Don't be such an old meanie."

"He knows you!" Attention made Jackie bold. She'd pay for this little mutiny later, but for now she desperately wanted to stay at the party.

Lennie Smith sauntered over. "Jackie-Sharon's-kid-sister! Where have you been all evening? Want to dance?"

Jackie couldn't believe the older kids were being so nice to her. "Can I?" she asked Sharon, breathless with excitement. Her first dance with a real boy!

Sharon dropped her arm from Jackie's shoulder. "You like her so much," she told Lennie, "you can adopt her. She'll bug you to death just like she bugs me."

"Give the kid a break. Anyway, she thinks I'm brainy." Lennie held Jackie's right hand straight out like he was priming a pump and see-sawed her around the room in an exaggerated polka. Jackie giggled so hard she couldn't stand up. The red-haired boy danced with Natalie in a similar fashion. Everybody was laughing, except Sharon. Jackie could feel the steam of her sister's fury thirty feet away.

When the record was over, Lennie left Jackie by the table and went to find his date.

"I've never had so much fun in my life!" exclaimed Natalie, flushed from her whirl around the floor.

"Me, either," Jackie agreed. "I bet even Angel and her friends aren't having this much fun."

Natalie scooped up a handful of M&Ms. "Phooey on Angel Allen. Who cares about her dumb old club?"

"We do." Sure, they were having a blast tonight with Sharon's friends, but on Monday they'd be back at Sidney Lanier with kids their own age. Angel's club was still the coolest thing at school. "You care just as much as I do. You're just not letting on," Jackie said.

Natalie pitched an M&M at her. It bounced off her cheek. Jackie retaliated, tossing an M&M at Natalie that landed in her hair.

"Fight, fight!" the red-haired boy shouted. He seized the bowl and fired M&Ms at the nearest girl. She picked a bunch off the floor and flung them back at him.

Soon everyone in the basement was throwing candy: M&Ms, candy corn, cinnamon red hots. Multi-colored pellets catapulted through the air. The girls squealed in the candy hailstorm.

Candy corn stings the most, Jackie thought, ducking under the table. The fight was so loud, her father would probably hurtle downstairs any second to break it up.

Her foot brushed a flat rectangular object. The thumbtack card with Mick Rowe's name painted in pink nail polish. Sharon would want to keep it as a souvenir of this night, provided they all weren't carted off to jail.

Suddenly the lights went out. Cloaked in total darkness except for the orangy glow of the jack o'lantern, the girls' yells escalated to shrieks. If someone got hurt, Sharon would really be in trouble. Although her sister wouldn't appreciate it and she certainly didn't deserve it, Jackie knew she had to get the lights back on, pronto. She crawled out from under the table. Groping her way along the wall, she tried to locate the light switch.

She bumped into something — no, two somethings that sprang apart. A boy yelled and Jackie realized she had accidentally kicked him. "I'm sorry — " she started to apologize when the lights came back on.

The two somethings were her sister and the boy Sharon had cornered by the furnace. The boy was massaging his bruised shin. Judging from Sharon's rumpled hair, Jackie suspected they had been kissing.

"You!" Sharon yelled, clenching her fists. "I might have known!"

"I didn't mean — " Jackie held the card out as a shield against her sister's wrath.

The boy took it from her. "Hey, that has my name on it! How come?"

Sharon plucked the card from him, her face crimson. "It's nothing."

"Sharon wrote it," Jackie said, attempting to repair the damage. Then, before she could halt the words, she blurted, "She wrote it because she's got a crush on you."

Chapter 8

The M&M fight altered the whole tone of the party. After the boys ran out of ammunition, they began shoving each other and acting goofy. The girls couldn't interest them in dancing any more. They stood in a disgruntled knot by the refreshment table, while their dates ignored them.

Jackie and Natalie went back upstairs, crunching M&Ms under their shoes, and watched television until Natalie's parents came. The party ended around eleven-thirty.

Without being told, Jackie went to bed, hoping to avoid Sharon as long as she could. Even though she and Natalie hadn't deliberately started the fight, Sharon was sure to blame Jackie for ruining her party. And she could hardly deny the fact that she had bumped into Sharon and Mick Rowe when the lights were out and spoiled Sharon's special moment.

Footsteps clicked-clacked down the uncarpeted hall. Her sister went into the bathroom to perform her nightly Noxema ritual. Jackie ticked off the minutes she had to live. She closed her eyes, unable to bear the sight of blood. But no one battered her door down. Instead, there were strange noises in the hall. What was Sharon doing, setting up a guillotine? In French class, Jackie had learned about Marie Antoinette being beheaded by such a contraption.

But Sharon went into her own room without so much as rattling Jackie's doorknob. Jackie couldn't believe it. She was off the hook tonight, but that only meant she'd get it twenty times worse in the morning. Plumping her pillow, she closed her eyes and let the quiet house wrap itself around her. At last she dropped into the uneasy sleep of a person who knowingly camped at the mouth of a rumbling volcano.

Jackie woke with an oppressive weight on her chest. The party. And Sharon's anger.

No way could she avoid Sharon today; it was Sunday. Maybe she'd get lucky and puff up with the mumps or some other highly-contagious disease Sharon hadn't already had.

She got out of bed. Revenge or no revenge, she had to go to the bathroom.

Outside her door a white line stretched between her room and Sharon's. Toilet paper! Someone had unwound a roll of toilet paper from the bathroom clear out to where Jackie stood. One end of the toilet paper had been taped to the wall between the girls' rooms.

Jackie followed the trail into the bathroom. The

line went right down the middle of the room, straddling the hamper, the bathtub, the sink, and even the toilet. The other end of the streamer had been taped to the toothbrush holder below the mirror, with Sharon's blue brush on one side and Jackie's green one on the other. What on earth . . . ?

"It's war," said a cool, controlled voice from behind her.

Jackie spun around. Her sister stood in the doorway. Even in her terry robe Sharon looked formidable.

"You scared me," Jackie said. "What are you talking about, war?"

Sharon folded her arms and stared levelly at Jackie. She didn't appear to be concealing a weapon. She didn't even seem particularly angry. Just . . . this strange unshakable coolness. "I've declared war on you."

"What do you mean?" This new calm Sharon unnerved Jackie more than the old haranguing Sharon ever did. Why didn't her sister scream at her and get it over with?

"Just what I said. After last night, I've decided I've had it with you. You are no longer my sister. As far as I'm concerned, you don't exist. I'm only talking to you now to give you the rules."

"What rules?"

Sharon pointed to the toilet paper trail. "This is the dividing line. You cannot cross it or dire things will happen to you. You are absolutely forbidden to come in my room or any part of the house that's on my side. If I catch you trespassing — "

"But I have to use the bathroom!" Jackie cried.

"You can't keep me out. This is *our* bathroom. We share it."

"If you'd look, you'd see I've divided everything in here, too. This is *your* half. That is *my* half." She yanked Jackie's sleeve. "You're standing on my half. Get over."

Jackie stumbled against the hamper. "What about the sink and the tub?"

"*That's* your half and *that's* mine," Sharon repeated.

Jackie stared at the strip of paper looped over the tub. "Are you crazy? I can't use half a tub! The water goes everywhere!"

"The *water* goes everywhere, but *you* don't," Sharon clarified. "When you take a bath, you can only sit in your half of the tub. Same with the sink."

"What about the shower? The faucet's on your side."

"You can turn on the water, but you have to stand in your half."

"But the water doesn't reach the back of the tub. How am I supposed to get wet?"

Sharon shrugged, unconcerned. "That's your problem."

This was insane! Did Sharon really expect to get away with such a radical plot? "How will you know I don't use your side?" Jackie asked.

"I'll know."

Her sister would probably pull a sneaky trick, like strategically placing a hair on her side of the tub or something.

"Listen, Sharon, I'm really sorry about last night — " Jackie began.

Sharon cut her off. "Save your breath. We're

at war and people at war don't talk to each other. Here are the rest of the rules. You cannot cross the battleline. You cannot touch my cat — "

"I don't *want* to touch your mangy fleabitten cat."

"You are only allowed to use the phone between four and six and only if I'm not using it. Tell your friends, if you have any, not to call after six or I'll hang up on them."

Jackie was outraged. "I can use the phone if I want to! I'm telling Mama! You can't do this!"

"Mom knows about the war. She said she's staying out of it. She's plenty mad at you and Natalie for messing up the basement. Guess who's going to clean ground-in M&Ms off the floor?" For the first time, Sharon smiled, smugly.

"It wasn't my fault! Natalie threw an M&M at me, and I threw one back at her, and then those boys started throwing them. We couldn't help what they did."

"Last night is over and done with. As of this minute, we are at war." She wheeled and left, like a general dismissing the troops. Jackie almost saluted.

Sharon meant business! But Jackie still couldn't believe her mother would actually permit Sharon to declare war on her own sister. Her mother would make Sharon get rid of that stupid dividing line, probably as soon as she got up.

The tube of toothpaste lay under the strip, separated from cap to bottom by the paper line. Careful not to stray over her side, Jackie squeezed toothpaste only from her half of the tube. In her part of the mirror, her face looked tense and drawn. The ravages of combat. Already the war was taking its toll.

Jackie was right about one thing: Her mother objected keenly to a streamer of toilet paper dividing her house. Sharon removed it, insisting it was still there, an invisible boundary like the Mason-Dixon line. As for the war itself, Mrs. Howard was steadfastly neutral.

At first the war didn't bother Jackie. She and Sharon frequently went through periods without speaking to each other. That was nothing new. And Sharon had barricaded Jackie from her room since last summer, so that wasn't new, either. What *was* different was the stillness from Sharon's side.

Jackie cleaned the basement floor, using a paint scraper to loosen squashed M&Ms and a rag to wipe up the chocolate dabs. The sagging orange and black crepe paper and the hollow-eyed jack o'lantern, all that remained of Sharon's party, made her feel sad. Sharon had planned the party and talked about it for so long, and now it was over. The day after Christmas her father always remarked that Christmas was as far away as it ever was. Sharon's party seemed like that, almost as if it had never happened. Since she and Sharon weren't speaking, they couldn't keep it alive by remembering bits of it.

On Sundays they ate dinner at one o'clock. Afterward the girls would do the dishes and then either they'd all go for a ride or their parents would take a drive, leaving the girls at home. More and more, Jackie and Sharon preferred to stay home alone, without their parents watching every little move they made.

Jackie had temporarily forgotten about the war as she took her place. Sharon sat down beside her, laying a ribbon between their plates.

"The line," she said tersely. "Stay on your side."

Battlelines even at the dinner table! Jackie glanced over at her father to see how he reacted to Sharon's ultimatum, but he was busy ladling gravy over his potatoes. Her mother passed him the chicken as if it were perfectly normal to serve a meal during a feud.

War complicated even the simplest tasks. Jackie discovered she could not pass the platter of chicken to Sharon without crossing the line. Likewise, Sharon was unable to hand her the potatoes. Jackie handed the platter back to her father who passed it over to Sharon. The process was reversed with the potatoes and gravy.

"I feel like an assembly line," Mr. Howard commented dryly. "I hope the United Nations negotiates a treaty soon."

"The quiet is kind of nice," Mrs. Howard said.

Jackie thought the war was awfully inconvenient. When Sharon accidently set her elbow on Jackie's side of the ribbon and then hurriedly moved, Jackie wondered if her sister was thinking the same thing.

After dinner, their parents decided to go for a drive by themselves, leaving the girls to do the dishes.

"Which half of the sink is mine and which is yours?" asked Jackie.

"You dry and I'll wash, like always," Sharon said.

"I'll try to stay on my side of the floor." Jackie picked up a plate Sharon had just rinsed. "Should I wipe the whole thing or just half?"

"Don't get cute." Sharon set a glass on the draining rack just as Jackie reached for it. Their hands brushed. Sharon yanked hers back as if she'd been burned. "Mom shouldn't make enemies work together," she said.

"Too bad we don't live in separate houses."

"If we did, we wouldn't be going through this," Sharon said, almost wistfully. Was her sister regretting her decision?

"We could stop," Jackie urged.

"No, we can't. I can't let you wreck my life any more. No more talking. People at war don't talk."

Sharon washed the dishes without uttering a syllable. Jackie dried, her own lips buttoned resolutely. They were quiet so long, her ears rang with the silence.

Whenever their parents left them alone in the house, it was customary to launch a "goody raid," an all-out attack on the kitchen cupboards to ferret out candy bars and cookies their mother hid from them. According to Mrs. Howard, she never had enough snacks to put in lunches because Jackie and Sharon inhaled everything not packed in mothballs. Jackie was insulted when her mother lumped her in the same greedy category as Sharon. She didn't eat *everything*, the icky green cherries in fruitcake, for example.

Goody raids were a long-standing tradition.

Jackie wondered if they'd have one today. Never mind they had just eaten huge slabs of apple pie or consumed at least a peck of M&Ms the night before at the party. Stolen goodies tasted the best. Jackie savored the fond memory of an ancient Almond Joy bar she'd once found behind the roasting pan. The nuts were as hard as peach pits, but at least she had struck pay dirt before Sharon that time. Her mouth watered just thinking about it.

Sharon's sugar craving must have equaled Jackie's because as soon as the last pot lid was put away, she nodded. The signal to raid the cabinets.

Following their familiar system, Sharon ransacked the corner cupboard, while Jackie leaped up on the counter to frisk the deep mixing bowls stacked on the top shelf where their mother stored bags of chocolate chips and other baking supplies.

Clinging to the handle of the cabinet with one hand, Jackie felt around the bowls. Nothing. She looked over to see if Sharon was having any better luck in the corner cupboard. Sometimes their mother kept peanuts and pecans up there. Sharon produced a linty lemon drop. That was it.

Sighing with disgust, Sharon stepped off the chair she used to reach the top of the corner cupboard, dusting her hands. Jackie climbed down from the counter. The goody raid had only lasted about ten seconds. Their parents would be gone at least an hour, probably longer. What would they do with all that time? Sunday afternoons were the worst, endless and boring.

Sharon disappeared into her room, firmly clos-ing the door. Jackie had no choice but to go into her own room. Through the heat register, she could hear her sister's television tuned to a movie. Sharon used to let Jackie watch her old TV. But not anymore and certainly not since the war had started.

Jackie contemplated her options. She could go into the living room and turn on the big set, but she didn't feel like it. Or she could work on her stupid guidance project. Time was running out. The report was practically due, and she still hadn't picked her subject, much less done the research. Homework didn't appeal to her, either. She thought about calling Natalie, but then she remembered Natalie was going to the mountains for the day.

Jackie decided to experiment with hairstyles. As she combed her hair, she wondered how long the war would last. In history she'd read about the Hundred Years War. Maybe theirs would last that long. She should be *glad*, really. In effect, the war was giving her a vacation from her mean sister. Learning to take a bath in half a tub was a minor drawback to being an only child.

Chapter 9

On Monday morning Sharon flipped past Jackie's room wearing her drill team uniform. It was a practice day; Sharon would come home late. She didn't speak and neither did Jackie.

Jackie was busy styling her hair. Sectioning off the hair on the crown of her head, she wrapped an elastic band around it, then teased the tail of hair so it formed a sort of waterfall. The tricky part was getting her hair to stay like that, which she accomplished with enough hairpins to set off a metal detector. But it was worth it. She looked totally different.

She walked slowly to the bus stop. With her new hairstyle, she had to be careful of running and high winds and open windows. Looking different made her nervous. Suppose the other kids laughed? Still, the only way to rise from the ashes of a Big Nothing and be Somebody was to become a whole new person. She'd start with her hair and gradually reinvent herself.

Natalie was waiting at their table in homeroom when Jackie breezed in, seconds before the bell.

"You almost didn't make it. Oh, your hair! I love it!" Natalie gushed. "It looks terrific. How did things go after I left Saturday night?"

Jackie sat down. "I had to clean the basement floor. Those M&Ms made a big mess."

"That's not what I heard," Natalie said mysteriously.

"How did you know Sharon declared war on me?"

"You mean, she didn't murder you for interrupting her famous love scene?"

"She's giving me the silent treatment. I can't go in her room or use her part of the bathroom or even put my elbow on her side of the table."

Natalie was amazed. "You guys are too much! When's it going to be over?"

Jackie shrugged. "Knowing Sharon, probably never. It's really not so bad. Kind of like not having a sister. Nobody yelling at me all the time, telling me to get out. I think I might even enjoy this war." She was beginning to feel like Somebody already.

Her confidence lasted until second period, p.e. class. As she entered the locker room, hoping Miss Cole would have a non-vigorous activity lined up like Tiddlywinks, she learned they were starting gymnastics. Playing tackle football in a hurricane couldn't mess up her hair any faster than doing headstands on a foam mat.

"Miss Howard," the teacher said after Jackie had performed a stiff-necked somersault. "Is there something wrong with your neck? You can't possibly do a forward roll with your head stuck up like a turtle's."

The class snickered. Jackie ducked her head between her knees and rolled, grimacing as hairpins clattered on the mat. Then she had to take a shower. By the time Jackie got to a mirror, she wanted to scream. The teased tail of hair on top of her head was standing up like she'd been electrocuted.

It was almost time for ESG. Rather than jockey for position in front of the steamy locker room mirror, Jackie raced to the girls' room closest to her ESG class where she had the mirrors to herself. With trembling hands, Jackie attempted to re-create the style. Why couldn't her stupid hair behave just this once, was that too much to ask?

Girls from the early lunch shift poured in, chattering and laughing. Claiming squatter's rights, Jackie refused to give her place to an eighth-grader. She ignored their stares as she frantically teased the tail of hair, then combed it into the soft waterfall, only it wouldn't *go* into a waterfall. Maybe she had teased it too much. If she kept fooling with her hair, it might break off and she'd have this huge bald spot on top of her head. The problem was, she couldn't brush her hair in the old style either. The elastic band had left a ridge so her hair wouldn't lie flat any more.

A group of seventh-graders came in. Angel Allen's perky face appeared in the mirror beside Jackie.

"Oh, hi," Angel chirped, digging in her purse for her brush. "Heard you had a great party Saturday night."

"Uh — yeah," Jackie stammered. How on earth did Angel know about Sharon's party? *Natalie.* Miss Western Union must have blabbed.

"It's all over school you danced with older guys all night, and things got pretty wild." Angel fluffed the ends of her waist-length hair.

"Well, it took me most of Sunday morning to clean the mess up," Jackie replied truthfully.

"Somehow I never thought of you as the party animal type. You seem so quiet."

"Still waters run deep," Jackie quoted her father, not really sure what the expression meant. What had Natalie *told* people?

"You know, I have this club — " Angel took the poodle barrettes out of her perfect hair and put them back in the exact same place. "I suppose you might have seen us around school. Anyway, the main thing about the club is that we're all interested in boys. We practice things, like how to act around them. I mean, next year we'll be eighth-graders, and we'll have dances — might as well get ready, right?"

"Right," Jackie echoed, wondering where all this was leading.

"There's room for two more," Angel went on.

Jackie grasped the rim of the sink, suddenly feeling woozy. Surely Angel wasn't about to let her in the club based on the rumor of a wild party.

"You have potential," Angel said critically. "If you'd like to be in the club, you have to prove you're really interested in boys — and that boys are interested in you. That's our only requirement."

Some requirement. It would be easier to win

the Nobel Prize. "How about Natalie McEvoy? She's my friend and she's absolutely crazy about boys."

Angel narrowed her eyes. "Is she? Well, we'll think about her." Then she seemed to notice Jackie's hair for the first time. "What did you do to your hair? Get bubblegum stuck in it or what?"

The bell rang and Angel left for ESG. Perspiration trickled down Jackie's spine as she tried one last time to fix her hair. Now she was even more nervous after her talk with Angel. She and Natalie were actually prospective candidates for Angel's club! Her hair was a lost cause. Giving up, Jackie stuffed hairpins into her purse and ran to class, even though she looked as if she'd gotten a terrible perm.

Miss Dale had already taken attendance. Jackie slipped into her seat, her face flaming. It was bad enough she had to barge in late without making an entrance like the Wild Man of Borneo.

"The warrior!" Daryl Forshay drummed the top of his desk. "Where'd you leave your spear? Cowabunga!"

During the break between English and social studies, Jackie collared Natalie out in the hall. "Angel heard about the party. And she's going to let us in her club!"

"Oh, wow! What do we have to do?"

"We have to prove we're interested in boys — and vice versa."

"Sort of like an initiation," Natalie said. "Well, that shouldn't be too hard."

Now that Jackie had time to consider Angel's proposition, she expressed her doubts. "I don't know if I like boys or not. I mean, I might like one boy, but *all* of them?"

"I'm sure Angel doesn't include turkeys like Daryl. Nobody's that desperate. But we'll do anything to get in her club, even if one of us has to *marry* Daryl."

"I draw the line at marriage," said Jackie. Actually, the one boy she considered liking *was* Daryl, but she'd never hear the end of it if she confessed her real feelings.

Jackie could almost see the lightbulb over Natalie's head. "I know! Suppose we just *pretend* we like all boys. After we get in the club, it won't matter."

"What about getting boys to like *us*. We can't fake that," Jackie said.

"Maybe we can," Natalie persisted. "What got Angel interested in you in the first place was the party."

"Which was your doing, wasn't it?"

Natalie modestly buffed her nails on her sweater. "Can I help it if Angel was lurking in the background when I told Susan Riley about the super time we had Saturday night? Anyway, here's what you do. Wear an old ring on a chain around your neck and tell Angel you're going steady with one of the guys you met at the party. A *high-school* guy! She'll fall all over herself letting you in the club, and then you can get *me* in."

"I don't have an old ring," Jackie said. "Just my birthstone ring and I'm only allowed to wear it on special occasions."

Natalie was undaunted. "What about something of Sharon's? When we were fooling around in her room the other day, I saw an i.d. bracelet.

In the drawer with her diary. Can't you borrow that?"

Jackie knew the bracelet Natalie meant. Walter Keaton, a former admirer now spoken of in derisive tones, gave it to Sharon in sixth grade. The bracelet was carelessly tossed in Sharon's vanity drawer along with her diary and a ton of junk. But it might as well be on Mars.

She shook her head. "I can't, Natalie. We're at war. If I put one toenail in Sharon's room, she'll kill me."

"Jackie! Are you going to blow our one and only chance to be in Angel's club over a measly technicality? Our seventh-grade reputation rests on this."

Then Jackie remembered Sharon had drill team practice. She could sneak into Sharon's room and take the bracelet before her sister got home. "All right. For Angel's club, I'll risk my life and cross the battleline."

The minute she was in the front door, Jackie went to Sharon's room. She tiptoed in, expecting alarms and whistles to go off any second. She eased open the vanity drawer. The i.d. bracelet lay on top of Sharon's diary. Jackie grabbed the bracelet and hurried out.

In the safety of her own room, she stuffed the bracelet under her mattress and then spent the evening worrying whether Sharon would rush in from drill team practice, announcing she had met Walter Keaton again after all these years and they were picking up where they had left off in sixth grade.

But nothing like that happened. The next morning, Jackie left for school wearing the heavy silver bracelet loosely around her wrist. In ESG, she dropped her pencil repeatedly to get Angel's attention.

"Klutz," Angel remarked, handing Jackie her pencil. At last she spotted the bracelet. "Is that what I think it is? Are you going steady?"

Natalie spoke up. "Yes, she is. He's wild about her."

Angel poked Marcia Rivett. "Jackie's going steady! See, some boy gave her an i.d. bracelet."

"Is he in our class? Does he go to Lanier? What's his name?" Marcia grilled.

"His name is — Walter Keaton," Jackie replied. "He's a junior at Fairfax." Well, he *was*.

"You're gong with a *junior*." Marcia practically foamed at the mouth.

"How thrilling!" Angel cried. "Did you meet him at the party Saturday night?"

"Well, we met once before." That was true, too. When Jackie was in the second grade, Walter came over to their house to help Sharon with her history project, a flatboat made out of popsicle sticks. He kissed Sharon on the cheek while they waited for the cooking tripod to dry. Sharon said later he smelled like Elmer's glue, and she didn't want him for a boyfriend any more. But she kept the bracelet.

"And he asked you to go with him at the party?" Angel prompted, conveniently providing Jackie with details.

"Yes!" said Natalie. "After one dance he told Jackie he couldn't live without her."

Jackie threw Natalie a dark look. "Sort of. He gave me this bracelet last night." The brazen lie nearly gagged her.

"Isn't it pretty?" Natalie thrust Jackie's arm out so Angel could admire the bracelet. To her horror, Jackie saw that the bracelet had turned inside-out and on the reverse of the polished bar was an inscription: *W.K. loves S.H.*

Angel pinned Jackie's wrist against the edge of her desk. "What's that say?" She squinted to read the initials. " 'W.K. loves S.H.' Who's S.H.?"

Jackie gulped. She never realized the bracelet was engraved! "Me," she said feebly. "I'm S.H." She couldn't very well be W.K., now could she?

"What's the S stand for?" Marcia demanded.

"My name, what else?" Her palms were slick. Lying always made her clammy.

Angel's gray eyes narrowed as she saw through Jackie's sham. "I thought your name was Jackie, short for Jacqueline. That's what you told Miss Dale the first day."

"My name is Jacqueline. I mean, my *middle* name is Jacqueline. But my first name, my *real* first name, is Samantha."

"Samantha Jacqueline?" Marcia jeered. "Come on! That can't be your real name. Who would name their kid Samantha Jacqueline?"

"Jackie's parents would, that's who," Natalie put in. "I think Samantha Jacqueline is gorgeous. You're just jealous because your folks couldn't think of anything but *Mar*-cia."

Actually, Jackie had no middle name. According to family legend, four-year-old Sharon, who had despised the idea of a new baby, was pacified by being given the honor of having two names all to herself. As Mrs. Howard explained it to Jackie, Jacqueline Howard was enough of a mouthful without further embellishment.

"You're lying!" Angel accused. "That's not your name, and I bet that's not your bracelet!"

"It is, too!" Natalie was clearly ready to argue all night, but Jackie knew they had lost.

"*Quelle stupide*," Angel said to Marcia with the assurance of someone who'd had eight whole weeks of conversational French.

"I have to go to the bathroom," Jackie said, sprinting up front to get the pass. The last thing she wanted was to start bawling.

Locked in a stall, she sobbed into a wad of paper towels. Why hadn't she examined the bracelet before wearing it to school? Now she'd never get in Angel's club, not after Angel and Marcia trapped her in such a stupid lie.

Jackie unbolted the stall and splashed cold water on her face. She dried her face and hands with more paper towels, which she crammed in the overflowing bin, then shuffled back to class, back to Angel's taunts. As far as Angel Allen was concerned, Jackie was still a Big Zip, a Nobody, not even a convincing liar.

It wasn't until Jackie was riding the bus home that she realized the i.d. bracelet was no longer dangling from her wrist. Panic-stricken, she dumped her purse upside-down, but there was no bracelet. It must have fallen off when she was in the bathroom.

The reality of the situation hit her like the proverbial ton of bricks.

Sharon's bracelet was gone.

Chapter 10

Jackie had once seen a Donald Duck cartoon where a dripping faucet kept Donald awake until he flew squawking out of bed, crazed by the annoying splat-splat which multiplied in his head to sound like cannon blasts.

On the not-nearly-slow-enough bus ride home, the significance of the missing bracelet doubled and tripled and quadrupled. Jackie understood how Donald Duck could be driven to destroy his entire house trying to stop a drip. If she could tear Sidney Lanier apart brick by brick to find Sharon's bracelet, she would and with her bare hands, too. If only she'd had time to run back into the girl's room, but ESG was the last class of the day, and she might have missed her bus.

Jackie shut her eyes against the horrible picture of the janitor burning Sharon's bracelet along with all the other trash in the incinerator behind the school. Tomorrow she'd scour the girls' room high and low. Maybe the janitor would forget to empty the trash can. Or maybe he'd turn the bracelet in to Lost and Found.

She half expected Sharon to pounce as soon as she stepped off the bus, the sheer heat of her guilt drawing Sharon like radar. Her sister was in her room, as usual. Sad music drooled through the heat register that connected their rooms. Sharon had been awfully quiet lately, and it wasn't just because of the war. Ordinarily her sister yakked on the phone or danced with her closet door or practiced her drill team routines. But for the past week or so, all Sharon did was hole up in her room and play maudlin songs.

As Jackie tossed her school books on her bed, a dreadful thought struck her. Suppose Sharon was pining away for Walter Keaton, her sixth-grade boyfriend? It was possible. Every now and then Jackie felt a twinge for Martin Johnson, a boy in her third-grade class she sort of liked. Martin sort of liked her back and told her so one day in the cloakroom when nobody else was around. Then his family was transferred and Martin moved to Turkey, leaving Jackie with a broken heart.

What if Sharon suddenly decided Walter Keaton was her true love after all, instead of Mick Rowe? She'd want to wear Walter's bracelet again, a reminder of what she'd had and lost. That would account for her sister's moodiness and the sad records. Sharon was probably pawing through her vanity right this instant, her vision blurred by tears as she rooted futilely for the bracelet. Then Jackie's door would suddenly splinter down the middle as Sharon forced her way through like the Incredible Hulk, the emptied vanity drawer in one hand and her drill team rifle in the other, demanding to know where her most prized possession was.

And what would Jackie say? That the token of undying love given to her by the boy she foolishly let get away was buried under a mountain of pizza crusts and dribbly milk cartons from the day's lunch?

"Jackie!"

She jumped at her mother's voice. "What?"

"Natalie's on the phone."

The clock on her nightstand read five to six. According to Sharon's strictly-enforced code of war, Jackie could use the phone another few minutes before curfew. She'd better hurry.

"How come you left without saying goodbye?" Natalie asked. "Are you mad at me because of what happened with Angel and Marcia? I did the best I could, but you could have *told* me the bracelet had Sharon's initials on it, and I would have come up with a better story — "

"It's not that," Jackie whispered. "I lost Sharon's bracelet!"

"What? Speak up. I can't hear you."

A shade louder, she repeated the grim truth. "When she finds out, she'll kill me. No, killing will be too good. She'll think of something really horrible."

"You worry too much, Jackie. I bet she hasn't even thought about that old bracelet in years. It was tangled in so much junk, I barely noticed it myself. How often does she write in her diary?"

"Not too often." Sharon had managed to make

a five-year diary last almost seven years, she wrote in it so seldom.

"Well, there you are. If she doesn't ever go in the drawer, how can she miss her bracelet?"

Natalie made it sound so simple, but then, she didn't have an ogre for an older sister.

The next day Jackie made a beeline to the girls' room near her ESG class, even before she went to her locker. Despite her crossed fingers, the janitor had not been lax in his duties. The waste basket was very, very empty. The rest of the room was clean as a plate.

Disappointed, Jacked trudged to the main office. Lost and Found consisted of a cardboard box stored under the counter. She asked the secretary if anyone had turned in a silver i.d. bracelet the day before.

"Not while I was here, hon," the secretary replied. "But you can hunt through the box if you want."

Her heart sinking, Jackie sifted through mismatched mittens and scarves, but found nothing even remotely resembling Sharon's bracelet. "Thanks anyway," she told the secretary.

Her last hope was Miss Dale. It was possible that Jackie hadn't lost the bracelet in the girls' room at all, but outside the ESG room. Her teacher might have spied the gleam of silver against the brown tiles and picked it up. The bracelet could be sitting in Miss Dale's top drawer right this very second, just waiting for Jackie to claim it.

She had two minutes before the homeroom bell, and she still hadn't been to her locker. Deciding her life was more important than the science book she needed for first period, Jackie ran to the English wing. In her mind she could see the bracelet, the heavy links curled against Miss Dale's key ring and a pack of gum the teacher had confiscated from Daryl Forshay.

Miss Dale was busy with her own homeroom. The class looked so different with other kids milling around, Jackie wasn't sure she had the right room at first. It seemed weird to see Miss Dale chatting with those strange kids, the same way she talked to her fourth-through-sixth period class. The teacher glanced up and saw Jackie hesitating at the door.

"Yes, Jackie? Can I help you?"

Suddenly shy, she gnawed at a thumbnail, a baby habit she thought she had conquered. "Did you find a bracelet in here yesterday? A silver one with writing on the inside?"

Miss Dale shook her head regretfully. "No, I'm sorry. I didn't find anything in the class yesterday except a rubber nose which I'm sure belonged to Mr. Forshay. I'll keep a look out for your bracelet, Jackie. It might turn up."

"Thanks." But she was more certain than ever that Sharon's bracelet was at the bottom of the incinerator, melted into an unrecognizable black lump, which was what *she* would look like after Sharon found out what she had done.

"How are you coming with your guidance project?" Miss Dale asked her.

Jackie couldn't meet her teacher's eyes. "I'm almost finished." She hated to fib, but what could she say? That she hadn't even started yet?

"Good. It's due at the end of the week, you

102

know. Your class seems very ambitious. It's exciting for a teacher to glimpse the wishes and dreams of her students."

Not this student. Jackie had evidently been behind the door when they were passing out ambition, and her most fervent wish at the moment was to have Sharon's i.d. bracelet clamped in her sweaty hand. The guidance project was only one more worry heaped on the tottering stack.

Jackie was late to homeroom, which earned her a dirty look from Miss Wood. She complained to Natalie about her lack of ambition. "I don't know what I want to be when I grow up. If I don't find that bracelet before Sharon misses it, I won't even *have* a chance to grow up."

"Forget about the bracelet and concentrate on your report or Miss Dale will give you a zero. That assignment is one quarter of our ESG grade. Just pick a topic and write the stupid report, for heaven's sake."

Jackie remembered how Robert Labson had simply reached into the yellow box and pulled out a folder at random. No wavering over subjects, no agonizing that the other reports would be better than his.

"Even if I had a topic, I couldn't get it done by the end of the week." Jackie chewed on her thumbnail again.

"Ask Miss Dale for an extension," Natalie suggested. "Tell her you've had to wait for a folder to be returned. I bet she lets you have another week."

Still, it was hard to face the fact that everyone in her ESG class had their future tidily mapped out, while she fussed over the most trivial decisions, like whether to part her hair on the right side or the left.

There was a seventh-grade assembly right before lunch. In the auditorium, Jackie and Natalie sat in the row directly behind Angel and the We Like Boys Club. Angel had brought sodas and two boxes of caramel popcorn to school. The girls passed the cans and boxes back and forth, as if they were at a Saturday matinee.

Natalie sighed. "If only we could get in that club."

If only! Jackie's whole life consisted of a long string of "if onlys." If only she had her guidance project ready. If only she and Natalie could worm their way into Angel's club. If only they were cool enough to be *asked*. If only she hadn't lost Sharon's bracelet.

"Is it possible to break out in a rash from worrying?" Jackie scratched her arm, which had suddenly begun to tich.

"Sure," Natalie said. "I think it's called hives or something. Don't tell me you're still frantic over that dumb bracelet?"

She didn't tell her. But she was.

At supper Jackie's itching had reached epidemic proportions. Her arms were red from scratching with the bristle side of her hairbrush.

"What's wrong with you?" her mother asked. Mr. Howard was working, so it was just the three of them. "You're digging like a hound dog over there."

"Maybe you need flea powder," Sharon said. Although Sharon wasn't supposed to speak to the enemy, she occasionally broke the code of war for an insult.

Mrs. Howard frowned. "That's not funny. Jackie, did you get poison ivy last weekend when you were fooling around in the woods?"

"No." After once rubbing poison ivy in her eyes, Jackie gave any three-leafed plants a wide margin. "It's just an itch. I can't stop scratching." She scratched her arm with a fork.

"Jackie!" her mother scolded. "If you're that miserable, you may leave the table. I'll look at your arms after I eat."

The conversation turned from Jackie's skin problem to something more vastly important, what Sharon would wear to the Homecoming dance.

"You should see the tough routine Miss Foster is having us do, flags tied to the ends of our rifles and everything. I'll have to change in the girls' locker room for the dance. A black strapless dress would be easier to pack and change into," Sharon added casually.

"Too bad you don't have one," Mrs. Howard said, equally casual. "How about your rust velveteen with the lace collar?"

"Oh, Mom, that dress is for old ladies. I want something new and dramatic. And strapless."

"No strapless! You're fifteen, not thirty."

"But I'll be sixteen in January! And everybody wears strapless dresses nowadays."

"Well, then, you'll stand out all the more covered up," reasoned Mrs. Howard. "Leave something to the imagination. It'll make you seem mysterious."

Glad the focus of attention no longer centered

on her and her rash, Jackie scratched and fretted over this new development. Sharon might go for the mysterious angle, instead of wangling a new dress out of their mother, and try on the rust velveteen with different accessories to get the proper effect.

Mrs. Howard got up to clear the table. "You better make your mind up to wear the rust dress."

"But I want a swirly dress to dance in!" Sharon protested. "How can I swirl in hot, clunky old velveteen?"

Sharon was probably already deciding on the just-right jewelry to wear with the velveteen dress, Jackie thought, her mind racing. Walter Keaton's silver i.d. bracelet . . .

"Who's taking you to the dance anyway?" Mrs. Howard asked.

. . . Sharon would run straight to her vanity and yank out the drawer, anxious to see how the bracelet would look with the dress . . .

"Carl Myers," Sharon replied, somewhat dolefully.

. . . She'd scrabble through rings and necklaces and old lipsticks, rabidly searching for her brace-let . . .

Her mother began running water in the sink. "Isn't he the one you went to the movies with that time?"

. . . And then she'd realize what had happened to her precious bracelet. She'd storm Jackie's room like Grant taking Richmond, with murder in her eye and her hands ready to mangle . . .

"I did it!" Jackie cried, leaping up so fast she knocked her chair over. "I took it!"

"Took what?" Sharon asked, forgetting they were at war. "What're you babbling about?"

"I took your i.d. bracelet." Jackie sobbed with relief. Nothing Sharon could do to her would be any worse than carrying that terrible secret burden a second longer.

"What i.d. bracelet?"

"The one Walter Keaton gave you. I took it to school and lost it!" Why was her sister taking so long to kill her?

"Oh, that old thing. I haven't worn it in years — " Now it was Sharon's turn to knock over her chair. "YOU WENT IN MY ROOM! YOU BROKE THE RULES! This calls for immediate retaliation."

"What are you going to do?"

"Take something of yours, what do you think?" Sharon marched to Jackie's room.

Jackie scurried after her, but Sharon slammed the door in her face. When she came out, after a great deal of noisy pillaging, she had an object concealed under her shirt.

"What do you have? You have to tell me. I told you about the bracelet, didn't I?" Jackie tried to grab it back.

Sharon dodged her easily. "Wouldn't you like to know?" she sang, going into her own room.

Chapter 11

Jackie was tired of the war.

The novelty of not speaking to Sharon had long since worn off. She didn't feel like an only child at all, something she thought she'd relish. Sharon was still *there*, a silent presence in the next room, formal as a boarder when they swapped places in the bathroom they shared. Jackie would ten times rather have Sharon railing at her than looking through her as if she didn't exist, but this was Sharon's war and Jackie couldn't do anything about it.

School was just as depressing. Jackie pleaded for an extension on her vocation report, which Miss Dale granted. But the price she had to pay for the extra week was stiff: Her grade automatically dropped one level. The best mark she could hope for was a B and that was highly unlikely. Disheartened, she retrieved the Forest Ranger folder from the yellow box and began her report. If her destiny was to wear an olive green uniform, then who was she to fight it?

She and Natalie seemed to have no chance at all to get into Angel Allen's club after the i.d. bracelet disaster. Angel and Marcia bragged about the fun things they did in front of the other girls in ESG, making the non-members feel like old shoes. Last weekend the club had a sleepover at Angel's house, and the weekend before they went roller-skating. Jackie hated the way she practically salivated whenever Angel even glanced in her direction. The two pink pencils in the clear plastic case clipped to Angel's ring binder tantalized her like a bone held just out of the reach of a hungry dog.

At lunch on the Friday her report was due, Jackie ate her submarine sandwich while copying the report over. Her handwriting slanted forward but she didn't care. She could only write rounded, up-and-down letters when she felt good about what she was doing.

Natalie proofed each mayonnaise-smeared page as Jackie finished it. "You keep spelling Yellowstone National Park *Jellystone* National Park."

Jackie snatched the paper back and erased the errors. Yogi Bear lived at Jellystone, which wasn't even a real place. "I'll never get done by two o'clock," she groaned. The report was twenty pages, double-spaced, but it might as well be a hundred.

"You still have to fill out the occupation sheet," Natalie said.

"Oh, that's right." Jackie had completely forgotten about that dumb questionnaire. She wasn't even sure where the ditto was. If she was very lucky and Miss Dale was in a good mood, she might pull a C on the project.

At the next table the We Like Boys Club was holding a meeting about Donnie Roebuck.

"Every girl in seventh grade has thrown herself at him," Jackie said. "I don't know why they bother. He's only interested in basketball, period."

"Do you believe this?" Natalie asked. "They're going to actually see who can get Donnie Roebuck first!"

"I thought they only practiced stuff with boys, like how to talk to them and stuff."

"I guess they've decided to have a trial run." Natalie picked the tomato slices off Jackie's plate. "You don't want these, do you?"

Jackie didn't have time to eat the rest of her lunch. "They might as well save their energy. Donnie hardly looks at girls, not even Angel."

"That probably makes it more challenging." Natalie added the tomatoes to what was left of her own sandwich. "Wouldn't it be a riot if someone *else* got Donnie Roebuck, somebody not in Angel's club."

"Who, for instance?"

Natalie smiled broadly. "Well, you for instance."

"Oh, no!"

"Or me." She leaned forward. "The thing is, we have just as good a shot at getting Donnie Roebuck as they do."

"You're overlooking one minor detail," Jackie said. "If by some miracle one of us got Donnie Roebuck, what would it prove? We're not in Angel's club, so who would care?"

"Angel would. She couldn't stand to have rivals. She'd make us members just to keep an eye on us, if nothing else." Natalie reached out and halted Jackie's pen. "We must decide right now if we're going to get Donnie Roebuck before one of them does."

"Right now as in this very second? Natalie, I have exactly forty minutes to copy over thirteen pages!" She wrenched her pen free. "Okay! I'll do it. Just let me finish."

"Who'll make the big play?"

"Not me," Jackie said. "If Donnie Roebuck hasn't looked twice at Angel Allen, he's certainly not going to fall for a future forest ranger."

"You never can tell. He may go for the outdoorsy type."

"Only if I slamdunked myself through a basketball hoop. Listen, I've put my neck on the chopping block twice now. First spying on Sharon and then swiping her bracelet. It's your turn."

"I'll make the sacrifice," Natalie said, holding one hand to her brow like a martyr. "After I get Donnie Roebuck and Angel asks me to be in her club, I'll insist you join, too."

"Fine."

"But I need your help," Natalie said. "In order to crack a stubborn case like Donnie Roebuck I'll have to be — irresistible. That's where you come in."

Jackie stared at her. "You want me to give you irresistible lessons?"

"Not you exactly. Your sister. Sharon's had dozens of boyfriends. She must know all about how to be irresistible."

"She also knows how to exterminate sisters in

111

three simple steps," Jackie replied. "We're still sworn enemies. Sharon hasn't said a civil word to me in ages."

"You don't have to talk to her. Or steal anything. Just read her diary. I'm sure it's chock full of tips on how she got all those boyfriends. If anybody knows about irresistible, Sharon would."

"Read Sharon's private, personal diary? Why don't you just shove me in front of a train? It'd be quicker and a lot less messy." The mere thought of such a foolhardy mission made her pen skip as she crossed a *t*.

"Jackie, it's our only hope. I don't want to miss another slumber party."

"How come Sharon is always our only hope?" Jackie asked. "There must be some other resources we haven't tapped yet. What about your mother?"

"My mo-ther?" Natalie's voice rose to an indignant screech. "What would my *mother* know about being irresistible?"

She had a point. Jackie's own mother knew all kinds of stuff like how to make gravy without lumps, and which lever to jiggle inside the toilet to make it quit running, but she wouldn't know the first thing about how to attract a boy. Sharon's diary was definitely a better bet.

"Do you suppose," Jackie mused, "the park service hires twelve-year-olds on the run from enraged sisters?"

Saturday evening, their parents went to the grocery store and left the girls at home.

Nervously twitching the curtains, Sharon watched the glowing red tail-lights of their car.

112

Jackie had never seen Sharon so distracted. When the car was completely out of sight, Sharon ran into her room, reappeared almost immediately with a paper sack, then locked herself into the bathroom. Very strange behavior, even for Sharon.

Jackie crept up to the door and listened. Sharon was filling the basin with water, which meant she was going to wash her hair. She'd be in there at least fifteen or twenty minutes. Plenty of time to find out how to be irresistible.

Felix was napping on Sharon's bed. He yawned at the intrusion, but he wouldn't give her away. Jackie went straight to the vanity drawer. The diary was under a jumble of plastic beads. The pink imitation leather cover was scratched from where Sharon had picked the little gold lock with a bobbypin after she lost the key. Sharon had slit the leather tab from the lock, unwittingly making her diary more accessible to desperate snoopers.

Oddly enough, she opened to the scribble marks she'd scrawled across an entire week in March years ago. She wondered why Sharon hadn't ripped the offending pages out.

The sound of Sharon's first rinse reminded Jackie to hurry. Quickly she flipped to later entries.

September 12: This boy keeps staring at me in English. I know he likes me. His name is Mick Rowe, and he's not jerky like the other boys. Linda says he's an egghead but he isn't. He's smart but not show-offy.

113

October 4: Mom said yes to the Halloween party! Linda and I are inviting mostly boys, Lennie Smith for her and Mick Rowe for me. Jackie and her dorky friend Natalie kept bugging us. Jackie demolished my best lipstick. If I smashed something of hers, Mom would make me pay it back the rest of my life. I didn't even tell Mom what she did. She'd let Jackie get away with it like she does everything else. The instant that kid was born, she could do no wrong. And I'm supposed to set a good example for her to follow, according to Mom. Who sets one for me? Nobody, that's who. I have to learn everything myself.

Jackie never expected to see her own name in Sharon's diary. She forgot all about the day she accidentally broke Sharon's lipstick, but apparently Sharon thought it important enough to write about. The next entry was November 1, the day after the disastrous Halloween party.

I'M SO MAD I COULD SCREAM!!!!! Jackie ruined — I mean RUINED my party! Linda turned out the lights like she was supposed to when she saw me and Mick over by the furnace. But just before then those stupid kids started an M&M fight and everybody went crazy. RIGHT when Mick was ready to kiss me Jackie kicked him so hard he had a huge bump on his shin. She *said* she was trying to find the light switch, but I know better. She did it on purpose! I hate her! I hate everything about her, the way she sleeps with her mouth open, the way she's always bawling every five minutes.

Did she really sleep with her mouth open? Yuck! Sharon wouldn't lie to her own diary. Her sister was dead wrong about the Halloween party, but Jackie knew there was no changing Sharon's mind once it was made up.

Things were ominously quiet in the bathroom. What was Sharon doing in there, using a whole bottle of shampoo? Jackie skimmed the pages, looking for some clue on how Sharon made herself irresistible to boys.

Wore my blue skirt today with the blue and cream sweater and Chanel cologne. Since Mick is kind of a serious guy, he'd be more attracted to class than flash. You'd think Halloween night never existed! He didn't say one word to me in English except "Hi." What is *with* that guy? He was certainly saying a lot more than "hi" when I cornered him by the furnace. How can he go from hot to cold? Maybe tomorrow I'll wear my tight black skirt and Charlie cologne like I always do and let him know I don't care two cents about him, even though it's not true.

Well, this was news! Jackie couldn't believe her eyes. Sharon, her pretty, popular sister, was actually being snubbed by the boy she liked! On the next page Sharon wrote:

I'm miserable! I asked Linda to ask Lennie Smith to ask Mick Rowe since they are in the same study hall what he thinks of me (Mick, I mean). And do you know what Mick said? He told Lennie "She's okay" just like that and went to lunch! I'm only okay! If I didn't like him so much I'd deck him!

Jackie was fascinated. She had never known one of Sharon's romances to turn sour. This explained the sad music and Sharon's preoccupation. Her sister was suffering from unrequited love, a fate worse than acne.

A sudden noise startled her. She spun around, flinging the diary to the floor.

Sharon swooped into her room like a gigantic vampire bat, the towel flapping around her shoulders. But the most shocking thing about her was her hair. Normally brown, it was now a revolting greenish-yellow and hung in lanky strands. Felix took one look and dived under the bed.

"Sharon!" Jackie shrieked, the larger issue at hand, that she had been caught snooping in her sister's diary, snuffed out of her brain like a candle flame in the wind. "What have you done to your hair? It looks like egg yolk!"

"I dyed it, which is what's going to happen to you. How could you be so low? Reading my private personal diary! Is nothing sacred in this house?"

Certainly not Jackie's life. Judging by the look on Sharon's face as she bore down on her, Jackie knew her days were numbered.

Chapter 12

Pushing past Sharon, Jackie streaked through the living room with only one goal in mind, to get as far away from her sister as physically possible. But as she skidded across the kitchen linoleum, it dawned on her she had run out of places to go. And Sharon was hot on her heels.

In a single bound, Jackie leapt up on the counter and clutched the handle of the "goodie" cupboard like a drowning man clinging to a rope. An Oh Henry bar or a few stray Oreos might save her. She'd throw them at Sharon, the way hunters in old movies tossed small animal carcasses to blood-thirsty lions to keep them at bay.

The force of Jackie's flying leap must have been too much for the flimsy cabinet door because the top hinge snapped like a matchstick. The door sagged like a shutter on a haunted house. She had actually broken the cabinet! If Sharon didn't tear her to shreds, her mother surely would when she discovered the cabinet door hanging by its bottom hinge.

Then Jackie realized Sharon was not at her throat. She hadn't even tried to follow Jackie into the kitchen.

She skinned down from the counter and went into the living room. Sharon was crumpled on the couch, crying as if the world was coming to an end. With her egg yolk hair exploding from her head, she looked as though it already *had*.

"Sharon, are you sick?" Jackie asked, cautiously kneeling beside the sofa. It could be a trick, but she didn't think so. Her sister absolutely never cried.

"My hair! I just saw it in the mirror over the TV," Sharon wailed. "It looks terrible!" In her misery, Sharon seemed to have forgotten the war.

Her hair did look awful. At this close range, Sharon's damp yellow head reminded Jackie of a half-dead chrysanthemum with the petals about to drop off.

"What did you do to it?" she asked.

"I tried to dye it blonde but it came out green! When Mom sees me, she'll probably shave my head!" This horrible image brought on a fresh wave of sobs.

Jackie couldn't understand why her sister had done such a dumb thing to herself. "How come you dyed your hair?"

"Why does anybody who isn't a blonde dye their hair? Honestly, Jackie, sometimes you're so dense!" Sharon's hair was drying in matted clumps and now she resembled a Chesapeake retriever after a long day mucking around in the marshes.

It suddenly occurred to Jackie that Sharon had bleached her hair to impress Mick Rowe, to reinvent herself much the way Jackie attempted to become Somebody by changing her own hairstyle. She was stunned by the revelation. Meanness aside, Sharon was just about perfect.

What a mess. Any second their parents would return to find the cabinet door swinging by two nails and Sharon with green hair. Not only that but when Sharon came to her senses and remembered Jackie had been reading her diary, she'd slaughter her. They both might as well start packing for Ivacota Farm.

"What am I going to do?" Sharon sobbed. She was actually asking Jackie for help! The magnitude of Sharon's problem made the war seem silly. Maybe this was how wars ended, Jackie thought, when fighting became pointless.

"You can always dye your hair brown again," she offered.

Sharon seriously considered Jackie's suggestion. "I probably could. Only I don't have any brown hair dye. Or any way of getting to the drug store before Mom and Dad get home. Sooner or later Mom will find out what I've done."

"Wear a scarf till then."

"All night? And all day tomorrow?" Sharon's eyes widened. "I hear a car!"

Jackie flew to the window. "It's them," she reported. "I have to do something quick." In the kitchen, she propped the broken cabinet door so it seemed normal. Of course, whoever touched the door next would be in for a surprise.

Sharon beat a hasty retreat to her room, leaving Jackie to meet their parents with what she hoped was a bland expression.

"What's Sharon doing?" Mrs. Howard asked immediately, thrusting a grocery bag in Jackie's arms. Her mother could positively smell trouble.

"She's in her room."

"Doing what?"

"I think she's sleeping. Did you get any good cereal?" Jackie asked, hoping to throw her mother off the scent.

"Asleep at seven o'clock in the evening? Is she sick?"

"She sort of has a headache." When their mother saw Sharon's hair, Sharon would ache all over.

Mrs. Howard bustled up to Sharon's room. Jackie followed, wishing she could warn Sharon.

Sharon was lying in bed with her head *under* the pillow instead of on top of it. Jackie's first impression was that her sister didn't have a head. She screamed. Sharon sat up, the pillow falling to the floor, and revealed her springy yellow hair. Then Mrs. Howard screamed. Sharon screamed when she saw her mother and made a grab for the pillow.

"Oh, my Lord! Tell me it's a wig." Mrs. Howard clutched the front of her dress as if she were having a heart attack.

"It isn't," Sharon replied dully.

"What *have* you done to your hair?"

"She dyed it blonde," Jackie said helpfully.

"It's not as bad as it looks," Sharon said to her mother.

"What do you mean it's not as bad as it looks! It's *green*! You've ruined your hair! Your father and I can't leave the house five minutes without you acting up. Bleaching your hair!"

If Jackie had been in Sharon's shoes, she would have started crying. But Sharon faced her mother squarely. "It was a mistake. I'll dye it back," she said. "If you'll run me up to People's so I can get some brown hair dye."

Mrs. Howard sighed. "I have a good mind to let you go around like that for a few days. Teach you a lesson. Get your coat on. And wear a scarf, for heaven's sake."

"What are you going to tell Daddy?" Sharon asked apprehensively. Jackie wondered herself. Most of the time Mr. Howard was easy-going, but a little thing like bleached hair could set him off like an atomic bomb.

"We won't say anything. If you get your hair back to its natural color, he doesn't have to know."

Jackie felt a bonding between the three of them. Even during this stressful time, the women of their family stuck together. Sharon didn't complain once when Jackie got in the backseat. In the hair dye aisle of the drugstore, Mrs. Howard and Sharon conferred over the color to choose, while Jackie fiddled with the swatches of fake hair. It could have been an ordinary outing to buy Sharon pantyhose.

At home again, they crowded into the girls' small bathroom to transform Sharon back to a brunette. Jackie handed her sister towels, feeling as if she were assisting a surgery. Sharon never once yelled at her for standing on her side of the bathroom. During this crucial emergency, the war was suspended.

After an application of Beautiful Brown permanent color, Sharon's hair wasn't exactly the shade she'd been born with, but it was near enough. She no longer looked like a Chesapeake retriever or a chrysanthemum.

"It's late." Mrs. Howard gathered soiled towels to throw in the washer. "And I haven't even put the groceries away yet. Jackie, off to bed."

The crisis over, Jackie changed into pajamas and got into bed. Sharon was the brave one, she thought. Bleaching her hair while their parents went to the store like it was nothing. Even if it didn't turn out so hot she *tried* it. Sharon was undeniably Somebody.

Jackie had drifted off into that strange place where she wasn't quite asleep, but she wasn't quite awake either, when she heard voices coming through the register. Her mother's sharp with anger. And Sharon's, thin but defensive.

She slipped out of bed, wrapping the quilt around her, and crouched by the vent.

" — don't know what's gotten into you lately," Mrs. Howard was saying. "First you ruin your hair and then you break the cupboard and leave it for somebody to get hurt! I just about brained myself when I opened the door and it fell on me!"

Jackie winced. The door she had propped so carefully had hit her mother in the head! Now Sharon would tell her she didn't know what she was talking about and her mother would stamp into Jackie's room to nail the true culprit.

" — sorry," Jackie heard Sharon mutter. "Take that out of my allowance, too, along with

Mrs. Cross's ceiling and the dye you bought for me tonight."

"I'm beginning to think we're giving you too much free rein."

"Too much!" Sharon said. "All I ever do is go to school and come straight home. Once in a while I have drill team practice. If it wasn't for the games I get to go to, I'd be crazy as a bat. You don't know what it's like to be stuck here in the sticks."

"I don't, do I? Where do you think *I* live, Paris, France? And I'd hardly call you deprived. You just went to Homecoming — "

"That I had to wear an old dress to."

" — and we let you have a Halloween party. What more do you want?"

Sharon's tone became bitter. "Other kids — my friends — go around after school."

"Where?"

"To Tops, mostly. They ask me to go with them, but I always have to say I can't."

"That teenage hangout at the Circle? Forget it, Sharon. After tonight I wouldn't press my luck if I were you."

"Why don't we live in town, closer to some action? I hate living way out here."

Mrs. Howard answered curtly. "If you think we're moving just to suit a fifteen-year-old snip, then you've got another think coming." She passed Jackie's room in a huff.

Jackie snuggled under the blankets again, but she couldn't sleep. Amazement left her staring into the dark. Sharon had actually covered for her, taking the blame for something she didn't do. But why? In her diary, Sharon said she hated Jackie. Tonight she'd had the perfect opportunity to get back at Jackie for stealing her bracelet and reading her diary and wrecking her party. But instead of pointing the finger at her sister, Sharon let their mother believe she broke the cabinet.

Jackie knew then what she had to do, even if it cost her the war. Growing drowsy again, she wondered how she could keep her mouth closed while she slept. She'd hate to gross everybody out drooling on her sleeping bag at Angel Allen's next slumber party.

The truce flag was actually an old undershirt tied to a carnival cane, but Sharon would get the general idea.

Jackie rapped on her sister's door and when Sharon said "What?" she opened it a crack and waved the flag. "Truce?"

"Well, if it isn't the scourge of the Western Hemisphere," Sharon said. "What do you want?"

"Can I come in?"

Sharon hesitated. "I guess." She was seated at her vanity, setting her Beautiful Brown curls on large rollers. She stared at Jackie in the mirror. "Well?"

Jackie twisted the cane in her hands. "I heard you and Mama talking last night. About the cabinet door? I was the one who did it."

"No kidding." Sharon wound a roller and secured it with a pink plastic clip.

"How come you didn't tell on me? Mama sounded pretty mad."

"Wouldn't you be mad if you went to put up

a can of soup and the whole cabinet fell on your head?"

"I didn't mean for anybody to get hurt. I was scared when I broke it, and that was the only thing I could think of."

"Don't worry. Mom would never dream her precious baby darling would do anything wrong. That's why she lit into me." Sharon got up from the vanity table and plugged in her dryer.

"Why'd you let her blame you? All you had to say was you didn't do it."

"Because." Sharon's tone was resigned. "I was tired of hassling. What was a broken cabinet door compared to bleaching my hair? When you get in trouble as often as I do, you learn not to sweat the small stuff."

This didn't make much sense to Jackie. She certainly wouldn't take the blame for something Sharon had done. "I still don't know why you let Mama believe you broke the cabinet."

"If I told her you did it, then she'd be on my back about not watching you while they were gone, that's why." With her hand poised above the dryer switch, she asked, "Is that what you wanted?"

"No." Jackie paused nervously. "I want to say I'm sorry for — for reading your diary. And also for taking your i.d. bracelet and losing it." The words finally out, she drew a deep breath. Sharon would accept her apology and everything would be hunky-dory between them again.

"I don't care about that dumb bracelet, but I'm still steaming about the diary," Sharon said. "You should never ever *ever* read another person's private thoughts."

"I know."

"Well, I hope you got your eyes full."

"I found out you hate me," Jackie said, feeling the knot that always preceded a crying jag clog her throat. The dam of tears burst. "You've hated me since the day I was born!"

"I don't hate you," Sharon said. "At least, not most of the time. But it's hard to like a sneak."

"I wouldn't have snooped in your stupid old diary or lost your bracelet if you paid any attention to me."

"I do pay attention to you. You're always in my room, like now. What am I doing if I'm not paying attention to you?"

"You never listen to my problems."

"What problems? How can a kid like you have any problems? You're not old enough."

"I am, too!" Haltingly, Jackie told Sharon the real reason she had read her diary, driven by desperation to get into Angel Allen's club, and how she and Natalie needed information they could only obtain from someone older. In the course of her confession, Jackie confided her worst fear: that she was doomed to misery in seventh grade — and probably for the rest of her life — because she was a Big Nothing. A babyish Nothing, at that.

"If you bawl every time somebody looks at you cross-eyed, no wonder the kids think you're a baby," Sharon said. But then she admitted, "I'm the youngest junior in Fairfax High. Most of the kids are sixteen or even seventeen. I'm the only fifteen-year-old. But I don't let it bother me. It never has."

"Because you're somebody special," Jackie

sniffed, wiping her nose on her sleeve. "You're on the drill team, and you go to dances, and you have lots of boyfriends."

"Yeah. Scads," Sharon said sarcastically. Jackie knew she was thinking of her failure with Mick Rowe. "Listen, I've known girls like this Angel Allen. You're wasting your time, Jackie. She'll never let you join her club."

Jackie suspected as much all along, but Sharon's observation caused her to sob again. "I'll never be popular like you! My only chance was to get in Angel's club."

"And maybe steal a little of her shining light?" Sharon shook her head. "It won't work. Girls like Angel only use people like you — borderline losers — to make themselves look better."

Jackie cried even harder. "I'll never be anything but a loser!"

Sharon ignored her hysteria. "Here's what you need to do. First, dry up! Second, you and Natalie start your *own* club."

Jackie snuffled. "Who'd want to join a club me and Natalie were in?"

"Make your club different from Angel's. Instead of having a club *about* boys, why don't you start one that boys can join? Go out on a limb a little."

Jackie gnawed her thumbnail as she thought about Sharon's theory. The problem with going out on a limb was that it might not hold her weight. Could she and Natalie start a club other kids would clamor to join?

There was only one way to find out.

Chapter 13

"Start our own club?" Natalie posed the question as if Jackie had suggested they buy an emerald mine. "But I was all set to go after Donnie Roebuck."

"What's stopping you?" Jackie said. "You'll have to be irresistible all by yourself, though, without any advice from Sharon."

They were in homeroom. This was going to be a short week, only three days. Thursday was Thanksgiving and they also had Friday off. If she could persuade Natalie that a club of their own was the ticket to popularity, then they could work on their strategy over the long weekend.

"Aren't you tired of chasing after Angel Allen?" Jackie asked. "I am. She'll never let us in her club so we might as well start one of our own."

"But who would join?" Natalie unskewered a magic marker pen from the spiral of her biology notebook and doodled arrows on the cover.

"You. Me."

"Wow. Two whole people. That's not a club. It's not even enough to play cards." Usually Natalie was more receptive. Jackie didn't understand why she was being so negative today.

"So, we'll ask people to be in it! We won't know until we try."

Natalie dealt her another potential problem. "Suppose they turn us down?"

"Then we'll ask somebody *else*." Honestly, pulling teeth was simpler.

"If we have a club," Natalie said, changing her tune slightly, "we need a gimmick, like Angel's pink pencils."

"We'll have to think about that," Jackie acknowledged. They *did* need a gimmick to attract members.

Natalie slumped back into her negative rut. "Angel already thought of the best gimmicks. Pink pencils, wearing pink on Thursdays. Not having any boys. We can't top that."

"I can't do it all by myself!" Jackie cried.

Natalie began doodling dots on the rubber part of her white sneaker. "This is going to be a big fat flop. Everybody will turn us down and we'll be the laughingstock of the seventh grade."

Jackie never realized beginning a club would be such an uphill battle. The trouble with Natalie was she didn't have any confidence. Jackie wasn't overflowing in that department either, but she figured if *one* person wanted to join their club, Natalie's usual optimism would kick into high gear.

Susan Riley walked by, heading for her seat.

Susan was okay. Not an "A" list girl like the ones Angel hand-picked for her club, but then neither were she and Natalie. Maybe it was time for the "B" list to band together.

Jackie spoke up. "Susan, how would you like to join our club?"

"Sure," Susan replied.

"See?" Jackie nudged Natalie. "The first person we asked wants to join."

Susan perched on the edge of their table, already chummier than Jackie had ever known her to be. "What kind of a club is it?"

Now that she had snagged a live one, Jackie had to come up with a gimmick, fast. The black polka dots Natalie had drawn on her sneakers filled her with sudden inspiration. "It's called the — the Lanier Leopards! All you need to be a member is a pair of polka-dotted tennis shoes."

Susan was eager but nobody's fool. She looked down at Jackie's plain white sneakers. "How come you don't have polka-dotted shoes? I thought this was a real club."

"It is," Jackie said hastily. "I'm waiting for Natalie to get done with her shoes so she can do mine." To keep Susan's interest from flagging, she added, "As a charter member of the Lanier Leopards, you get customized tennis shoes. Natalie will draw dots on yours, too."

"Okay." Susan seemed pleased. "When do we have a meeting?"

"Today at lunch." Then she thought of a can't-fail gimmick, even better than polka-dot tennis shoes. "We're having a membership drive. Anybody can join our club so bring a friend."

"Anybody? Even boys?"

Natalie colored an enormous dot on the toe of her right shoe. "The Lanier Leopards Club," she said importantly, "doesn't exclude anyone. *Especially* boys."

By lunchtime both Jackie and Natalie were sporting polka-dotted tennis shoes. Kids in the food line stared at their feet, and a couple asked why they were wearing spotted tennis shoes. Natalie went right into the spiel they had concocted in the last few minutes of homeroom, about how the Lanier Leopards was a club to promote seventh-grade spirit, no matter how lowly the elitest eighth-graders tried to make them feel.

"After all," Natalie proclaimed, warming to her subject. "Where would the eighth-graders be without us? They couldn't very well be number one if they were the only class in the whole school, now could they? They were seventh-graders *themselves* just last year."

Daryl Forshay plopped his tray down at the table where Susan, Natalie, and Jackie were sitting. Robert Labson sat down across from him.

"I hear you guys have a new club," Daryl said. "And *anybody* can join."

"Well, yes, but — " Natalie faltered. Jackie knew she was racking her brain for a graceful way to say "anybody but you."

"Too bad," Daryl said bluntly. "I started a new club myself. It's called the We Hate Girls Club but nobody wanted to be in it."

"I can see why!" Jackie giggled. Daryl's answer to Angel's snooty club was even better than theirs.

"Since our group was a bust, we've decided to join yours." Daryl reached over and helped himself to a dill pickle from Jackie's tray.

Jackie looked at Natalie. If Daryl and Robert wanted to join, they couldn't say no. She and Natalie knew only too well how it felt to be shut out.

"Are we in?" Robert asked her.

Jackie remembered how Robert had chosen his topic for the vocation report, as if he didn't care. But now his brown eyes were anxious. It was tough always being on the outside of things.

"Have you got some old tennis shoes?" When he nodded, she said, "You're in."

They had five members! In a short time, the Lanier Leopards had gone from two to five. Five was a number that people couldn't ignore, a number to be reckoned with.

"So." Daryl popped an olive from Jackie's lunch into his mouth. "What do Lanier Leopards do besides run around in polka-dot tennies? I know! We can eliminate the eighth-graders one by one. Like this." He pretended to strangle Jackie. "Cowabunga!"

Jackie broke away from his grasp and swatted at him. She was flattered by his attention, but of course she had to act like she wasn't. No matter what kind of a club the Lanier Leopards turned out to be, it certainly wouldn't be dull with Daryl Forshay around. Life in the seventh grade was starting to look up.

By Wednesday, there were nine members in the Lanier Leopards, all wearing polka-dot tennis shoes. The fad caught on like wild-fire. Jackie never realized the power of starting a trend. Kids she barely knew were calling to her in the halls. Even Donnie Roebuck said hi on his way into Mrs. Nicely's science room. Stunned, Jackie walked right into a wall.

When Jackie told Natalie, her friend nearly burst with excitement. "If he noticed you, he'll notice me! Jackie, this club was the best idea!"

Things were going so well, Jackie didn't even flinch when she got a D+ on her guidance report. She had no intention of becoming a forest ranger when she grew up. She'd probably change her mind fifty times before she decided what she'd be. That was okay; she had lots of time.

During lunch, the Leopards sat together near the We Like Boys Club. Daryl, the Human Garbage Disposal, stole tidbits from everyone else's tray, prompting Susan to suggest they have a picnic when they came back to school from the holidays.

"No turkey leftovers," Daryl said. "Only good stuff allowed."

A picnic right in the middle of the cafeteria! Jackie listened to the plans being made around the table as they decided who would bring what to the first annual Lanier Leopards Post-Thanksgiving No-Turkey Picnic. Such an event would attract even more kids who'd want to belong. The club was a success!

The We Like Boys Club seemed subdued, their secret whisperings drowned out by the boisterous Leopards. Jackie sneaked a look at Angel. The queen of the seventh grade glumly ate her lunch, surrounded by her loyal subjects. Jackie pictured all the other girls in their class joining the Leopards, and Angel holding up the last two pink and silver pencils as she begged someone — *any*one — to be in her club. The thought made her feel good.

No, better than good. Wonderful.

Thanksgiving at the Howard's house was a quiet, small affair. The year they moved into the new house, when Jackie was five, they invited the Martins, the childless old couple who lived next to them, to share the occasion. That was the year Sharon taught Jackie to say a special grace.

When her mother called on her to do the honors, Jackie folded her hands, bowed her head and recited, "Good bread, good meat, good grief, let's eat."

Jackie's mother blanched while the Martins looked as if they'd tumbled into a nest of heathens. Sharon sputtered with pent-up giggles. Mr. Howard made Jackie apologize, said a proper grace himself, then calmly explained to their guests as he carved the bird that, despite their sweet demeanor, his daughters were no angels. The Martins agreed a bit too readily.

Since then they ate dinner alone, just the four of them. The Martins politely refused further invitations, claiming they preferred to eat at a restaurant, but Jackie suspected they couldn't stand another meal with her and Sharon slapping each other under the table.

Thursday morning, Mrs. Howard got up at the crack of dawn to start the turkey. Sharon stayed in her room, still moping over Mick

134

Rowe's rejection. Jackie helped in the kitchen until the Macy's parade came on television, which she loved to watch. She debated asking her sister to watch the parade with her.

After their heart-to-heart, Jackie thought the war was over, but Sharon still kept to herself. Jackie wanted to forget about the stupid war and watch TV together the way they used to.

"The parade's on," Jackie said enticingly outside Sharon's door. "There's a new balloon this year. Olive Oyl."

Sharon didn't reply.

Disappointed, Jackie switched on the set in the living room. The parade wasn't nearly as much fun without Sharon making snide comments about the marching bands and the girls riding on floats. Jackie went back out to the kitchen, where her mother was dicing celery for the dressing.

"Tell Sharon to get her tail in here and help. I can't do this dinner all by myself," Mrs. Howard said.

"Sha-ron!" Jackie hollered from the kitchen. "Mom says come help!"

Her mother pursed her lips. "*I* could have done that."

Sharon shambled in, red-eyed and sullen. Jackie wondered if her sister had been crying. "What is it? I'm busy."

"You're no busier than I am," Mrs. Howard said crisply. "Wipe off the good china. And get down our good stainless."

Sharon brought the wooden flatware box down from the corner cabinet. "Why do we have to eat dinner at home every year? Why can't we go out to a restaurant for once? It's more sophisticated."

"Yeah!" Jackie jumped in. "McDonald's! Can we go to McDonald's instead?"

"Eating at home is so tacky," Sharon continued, as if Jackie wasn't there. "I wish we could dress up and go to Sir Walter Raleigh's and have surf and turf."

"Steak and lobster on Thanksgiving! Families are supposed to eat at home," Mrs. Howard said. "It's tradition."

Jackie thought back to her fifth-grade history class. "The Pilgrims ate raw pumpkins and cranberries and squash — "

"Gross." Sharon wiped four silver-rimmed china plates with a clean tea towel. "If I were a Pilgrim and I had to eat raw pumpkin, I'd catch the next boat back to England."

"A Big Mac would definitely taste better," Jackie said. "Don't you think so, Sharon?"

"Are you two on speaking terms now?" Mrs. Howard wanted to know.

"Sort of — " Jackie said.

"Not exactly — " said Sharon at the same time.

Mrs. Howard finished mincing the celery and started on the onions. "You ought to be ashamed of yourselves, fighting during the holiday season. One of these days you'll realize life is too short for such foolishness."

Jackie looked over at her sister to see if their mother's statement had any effect on her. Warring countries declared a cease-fire during holidays. Both sides would lay down their weapons and stop fighting for twenty-four hours. She and

Sharon didn't have any weapons to lay down. They weren't out-and-out fighting . . . just — not getting along.

"What have you girls got lined up for tomorrow?" Mrs. Howard asked.

"Natalie and I are having a meeting on the phone tomorrow," Jackie said. "To get our club organized."

"How did you ever come up with a name like the Lanier Leopards?" Her mother chatted as if nothing were wrong between Jackie and Sharon.

"I thought of the name just like that," Jackie said. "But Sharon was the one who said we ought to start our own club, instead of trying to get in Angel's. It worked out great."

"Sharon has a lot of good ideas," her mother agreed. "I'm glad you're finally realizing that about your sister. Being bigger means you know more, isn't that right, Sharon?"

"Oh, yes, I'm such a fountain of wisdom," Sharon said wryly.

Being bigger, Jackie decided in the warm, fragrant-smelling kitchen, also meant being bigger-hearted.

Sharon didn't have to advise Jackie to start her own club. She could have just as easily told Jackie to take her problems someplace else. Sharon's self-confidence was rock-bottom. Maybe if Jackie reminded her that she was Somebody, she'd cheer up. Jackie could tell a story about one of the many times Sharon had got her but good.

"Sharon, do you remember the time Mama and Dad went to the store and you were supposed to watch me? You were on the phone and

I wanted you to play with me. Then you said there was this big gorilla coming up the driveway and I ran and hid in my closet."

Mrs. Howard laughed. "You mean you actually believed her?"

"Jackie is incredibly gullible," Sharon said. "She believes anything you tell her."

Jackie went on. "I waited in the closet for Sharon to say the gorilla had gone. I waited and *waited*. Finally I went out and Sharon was still on the phone, laughing! She only made up the gorilla to get rid of me! Remember that, Sharon?"

"You bring up the stupidest stuff." Her sister set the table without sparing her a glance. But she smiled, just a little, remembering.

Chapter 14

The Saturday after Thanksgiving it snowed. Jackie woke up to seven inches on the ground and more falling.

Her mother was lingering over a cup of tea but her father had left for his part-time job at Weber Tire Company. He wouldn't be home until very late, after a long day of putting snow tires and chains on cars. An early snow almost always took people by surprise.

Jackie bounded out to the kitchen in her pajamas. "Can we make snow cream?"

She already knew the answer, but she had to ask anyway. It was tradition, like Thanksgiving dinner. Her mother would undoubtably say they couldn't make snow cream from the first snow of the year. Or the snow wasn't deep enough or it hadn't been cold enough to kill all the germs in the air. The conditions for making snow cream were so specific and exacting that Jackie had only had the rare treat once in her entire life, the winter they moved into the new house.

There'd been a terrific snowstorm that January. Schools were closed for two weeks. Jackie hadn't started first grade yet so she wasn't missing anything, but she was delighted to have her big sister home on an unexpected vacation. The days Sharon went to school were endless for Jackie, who had to amuse herself watching cartoons and playing by herself. Sharon persuaded their mother to make snow cream, a delicacy Jackie had never even heard of.

They went outside and scooped up snow in a bowl and took it inside to their mother. Working very quickly, Mrs. Howard stirred in sugar, vanilla, and cream. The girls dipped their spoons in the bowl. One bite sent an exquisite pain shooting to Jackie's temple but she ate as fast as Sharon. Jackie would never forget the memory of that delicious cold sweet stuff melting on her tongue. Nothing in the world, not even a Baby Ruth bar hidden in the cupboard, tasted as wonderful as snow cream.

This year Mrs. Howard had a new excuse. "You're too big for snow cream," she said. "That's for little kids. Anyway, I don't think the snow is clean enough any more. I don't trust it."

Too big meant too old. Suddenly Jackie had crossed a dividing line she wasn't even aware of, being too old to ask for snow cream. It was like being too old to go trick or treating — another ritual knocked out from under her. If she couldn't have snow cream, then what good was snow to her now? It was just a nuisance, something to dread every winter, except for the bonus of school closings.

"Well," Jackie said with as much dignity as she could muster. "I guess I'll go in my room and read up on foreign policy."

Her mother laughed. "You are so funny! You're just like Sharon was at that age, wanting to be a kid one minute and a grown-up the next."

"Really? I thought Sharon was born old. I bet her first words were about a black strapless dress."

"Sharon had to learn it all the hard way. She didn't have an older sister to help. You can benefit from her experience."

If I live that long, Jackie thought.

Felix materialized from out of nowhere, as was his habit, and nosed around his empty cat dish. Since he slept with Sharon, his appearance meant that the Queen of Sheba was finally up. She came out, yawning and dragging the cord belt to her ratty old bathrobe.

"Snow," Sharon said, as if she were reading the word off a flash card written in big block letters. Jackie wondered if growing older meant you began to lose contact with the real world.

"Yes, snow." Jackie pretended to define the word the way Miss Dale did in vocabulary. "Cold white stuff that drops from the sky and piles up and has to be shoveled. No two flakes are alike."

"That's for sure." Sharon scuffed over to the stove to make herself a cup of tea. "Mick Rowe shovels snow with his father. He has his own truck and a plow and everything. He told me once he hoped it would be a snowy winter so he could make a bundle."

"Maybe he could come plow our driveway," Mrs. Howard said. "Daddy won't be home till late, and he might have trouble getting the car up the hill."

"Well, get somebody else!" Sharon said. "I wouldn't ask Mick Rowe to plow our driveway if we were buried under twelve feet of snow!"

"If we were buried under twelve feet of snow, we wouldn't need a plow," Jackie said. "We'd need a machine that makes tunnels because — "

"Will you make her be quiet?" Sharon asked Mrs. Howard. "It's bad enough I'm stuck in this wasteland without having to put up with her, too!"

She took her tea back to bed where she could be miserable among the comfortable debris of her own room. Jackie thought about the other times they'd been snowed in and how she and Sharon would build snowmen and throw snowballs and have fun. It was going to be a long, long winter.

Still, Jackie hated to see her sister so unhappy. Sharon had helped her by suggesting she start her own club, and it had worked out super. Jackie was actually Somebody at Sidney Lanier Junior High. She might even be as popular as Sharon by the time she got to high school.

It was time to return the favor. And she knew exactly how to do it.

She went into the hall and lifted the phone book off the shelf under the phone table. There was only one Rowe listed in the Fairfax area, that had to be his family. Making her voice sound as adult as possible, she spoke to Mrs. Rowe, Mick's mother, and requested "the boy" to plow their driveway. Mrs. Rowe promised to add the Howards to her son's list of clients. Jackie hung up, pleased with herself. Mick Rowe would soon be in their very own driveway.

She hovered around the picture window in the living room the rest of the morning. It had stopped snowing, but there was very little traffic creeping down Lee Highway. The orange state snow plow trucks would soon be by to clear the road, armies of them that Jackie would hear thumping and rasping all night. At the moment, she was interested in one particular snow plow.

Jackie left her post only to wolf down a peanut butter and jelly sandwich.

"What's so fascinating out the window?" her mother asked.

"Nothing." After Mick arrived would be time enough to let her mother know she had hired someone to clean their driveway. She hoped he charged reasonable rates. He ought to do the job for *free*, the awful way he'd treated her sister.

At two-thirty a battered red truck paused at the bottom of the hill. The person inside the cab lowered the blade and began scraping the driveway.

"Who on earth is that?" Mrs. Howard said, looking out the window. "You don't suppose your father asked one of his friends to take care of our driveway while he worked today?"

"He didn't, but I did," Jackie confessed. "I called Mick Rowe — you know, that boy Sharon was talking about? — and hired him to do it."

Predictably, her mother went up like a signal flare. "Young lady, since when do you make family decisions?"

"Since — since I'm too old to have snow cream!" she rationalized. "Mama, it's for a good cause! I did it for Sharon. You were going to call somebody *any*way. What difference does it make who dialed the phone?"

"I don't care what cause it's for! You and Sharon both take entirely too much upon yourselves. Next you'll be running the house. You're getting to be as headstrong as Sharon."

Her mother's criticism was music to Jackie's ears. She was headstrong, too! Not Big Nothing Bawlbaby, but Somebody who took charge and made things happen!

"Yell at me later," she told her mother, bundling up in her coat and boots. "I have something important to do."

Mick Rowe was plowing the turn-around part of their driveway when Jackie waved at him to crank down his window. He looked handsome in red knitted cap and muffler, not at all like a loutish brute who would deliberately hurt her sister.

"Hi," he said. "I remember you from the Halloween party. At least, my shin hasn't forgotten!"

"Maybe your shin hasn't, but the rest of you has," Jackie said tartly. "How come you don't like my sister any more?"

"Who said I didn't like her?"

Jackie didn't want him to know she'd been snooping in Sharon's diary. "Well, you haven't been back since the party. If you like somebody, you come around."

Mick leaned out of the cab. "I'll let you in on a secret. I like your sister a lot. But she's so popular, I don't stand a chance competing with all those other guys buzzing around."

Jackie was speechless. It never occurred to her that Sharon's popularity would act against her with the boy she liked the most. "Those other guys are just — guys," she said, aware she wasn't helping the situation any. "You don't have to worry about — "

"JACKIE HOWARD, GET IN THIS HOUSE!" Sharon bellowed from the carport.

Mick's face brightened when he saw her. "Hey, Sharon! Ride with me while I finish your driveway."

"I can't," Sharon said haughtily. "I'm not dressed to wade around in the snow." She was wearing her best pants tucked into knee-length boots, a cable-stitched sweater and a tasseled cap on the back of her head. She looked like Elizabeth Taylor in *National Velvet*. No one would ever suspect she had been slopping about in a torn bathrobe just moments before.

Jackie piped, "If she won't ride with you I will!"

"I THINK I CAN MAKE IT OVER THERE!" Sharon struck out across the yard like Lewis and Clark on the last lap of the Northwest expedition. Sharon mushed through the snow as if she were leading a dog sled team, then paused daintily by the truck until Mick unlatched the passenger door and helped her in.

"You want to ride, too?" Mick asked Jackie.

Sharon threw Jackie a meaningful look. Jackie winked at her sister. Not a very good wink, because Jackie had never learned to keep her other eye from blinking, but Sharon got the message. She grinned at Jackie.

"Some other time," Jackie told Mick. "You two kids have fun." She went back in the house, mission accomplished. Whatever misunderstanding Mick and Sharon had would be straightened out now, within the cozy confines of his heated truck.

"Did you ever hear of being too popular?" Jackie asked her mother, who was putting the teakettle on for hot cocoa. Even if she hadn't hired the snowplow person herself, she would still offer him a hot drink. "That was why Mick and Sharon weren't getting along. He thought she was too popular to like him, and she thought he didn't like *her*. Isn't that crazy?"

"I suppose it happens," her mother said. "Popularity can scare some people off. You ought to remember that when you start making a lot of friends."

"No danger of that." Even if the Lanier Leopards had a hundred members, Natalie was Jackie's best friend. Maybe even her best-best friend. Natalie knew her when she was a bawling nobody. If Natalie tolerated her *then*, she was a true friend.

Mick finished the driveway and came in for hot chocolate. From the way Sharon hung possessively on his arm, Jackie knew they had more than made up. Then Mick left to go on to his next snowplow job. Jackie figured her sister would call Linda first thing and let her in on the good news. Instead, Sharon went into her room.

Jackie hesitated by the door. Sharon was busy writing in her diary. She waited until Sharon put the pen down, then said, "Are you Mick's girlfriend now?"

"Yes! He asked me to go steady! It was so romantic in the truck with the snow all around and everything. He's going to bring me his class ring Monday when we go back to school. I'm so happy!" She picked up Felix and spun him around. When she put the cat down on the floor, he staggered in uneven circles, as if he were still spinning.

Jackie laughed. "He looks like he's drunk."

"He is drunk! We're all drunk! Drunk with love!" Sharon flung open the window over her bed, letting in a refreshing blast of chilly air. "I'm in love, do you hear!" she screamed in the direction of the Martins' house.

"They probably don't care," Jackie said. Sharon was acting like Ebenezer Scrooge on Christmas morning when he realized he had been given a second chance. So this was love! She wished she could feel like Sharon. Daryl Forshay was probably not going to be the one to cause Jackie to throw open windows in the middle of a snowstorm, but she guessed love would come eventually.

"Sit over here," Sharon said. "How deep do you think the snow is?"

"About seven inches." She felt funny sitting so close to her sister, after so many weeks of glancing off each other like magnets turned the wrong way. Felix jumped up and teetered on the windowsill, confused to find the window open.

"It's pretty, isn't it? I never realized how beautiful snow is." Sharon got up to slide her vanity drawer out. She brought it over to the bed. "I think it's time I cleaned out this drawer."

"Right now?" Jackie giggled. "What are you going to do, throw the stuff out the window?"

"Yes. Want to help?"

It was such a crazy impulsive thing, just like the old days when Sharon would dream up some wild scheme, like goody raids.

Sharon plucked an old lipstick from the tangle of junk and tossed it out the window. It landed in the soft powdery snow and dropped out of sight, leaving a tube-shaped hole. "Oh, that's pretty! I wonder what a barrette would look like." She threw a hair clip out the window, which left a hairclip-shaped impression next to the lipstick tube hole. "You do one."

Jackie selected a strand of glass beads. She flung the necklace with abandon. "This is fun! I'm sorry I lost your i.d. bracelet. It would have made a neat design."

"That's okay," Sharon said generously. "We've got plenty here to pitch."

"Are we still at war?" Jackie asked.

"Only if you want to be." But Sharon sounded reluctant.

"No, I don't." Thinking of the bracelet reminded Jackie of something else. "What did you take from my room that time, you know, to get back at me?"

Sharon grinned. "Nothing. I just pretended

to. We had to stick to the rules or else it wouldn't have been much of a war."

She didn't *think* Sharon had stolen something of hers in retaliation. She had searched high and low but never found anything missing. Maybe her sister really wasn't so mean, after all.

"I'm glad you have your own club at school," Sharon said.

"And I'm glad you and Mick are going steady." Sharon didn't thank her for bringing them together, but she didn't have to. Fishing for gratitude would show a definite lack of class. For the first time, Jackie felt like Somebody in her own house.

The war had let her experience being an only child, sort of. She found she didn't like it. Whatever problems she and Sharon had, she wouldn't trade her sister for anything. Well, almost anything. She hoped no one would tempt her with a romantic evening with Donnie Roebuck.

To commemorate the end of the sister war, Jackie threw an empty perfume spray into the air. "I'll never forget this day as long as I live," she said.

"Twenty years from now you'll tell me about it," said Sharon. "You're always bringing up the weirdest stuff."

"Is that so bad?"

Her sister smiled. "I guess not."

Together they tossed objects out the window, old compacts and earrings, gluey lipsticks, and calcified bottles of nail polish, into downy deep snow below and watched new patterns bloom like stars.

About the Author

CANDICE FARRIS RANSOM, born July 10, 1952, is a younger sister. Many of her stories, including the popular Kobie books, *Going on Twelve*, *Thirteen*, *Fourteen and Holding*, and *Fifteen at Last* are based on her own experiences growing up. Ms. Ransom says, "My brain stops at about age fifteen. I'm a grown-up by default."

Raised in Centreville, Virginia, Ms. Ransom still makes her home there with her husband, Frank, and one cat. *My Sister, the Meanie* is also published in hardcover. Ms. Ransom has written thirteen books for young readers. She is currently working on two more books for Scholastic about the trials of sisterhood shared by Jackie and Sharon.

APPLE PAPERBACKS

Pick an Apple and Polish Off Some Great Reading!

NEW APPLE TITLES

❑ MT43356-3	Family Picture	Dean Hughes	$2.75
❑ MT41682-0	Dear Dad, Love Laurie	Susan Beth Pfeffer	$2.75
❑ MT41529-8	My Sister, the Creep		
	Candice F. Ransom (May '90)		$2.75

BESTSELLING APPLE TITLES

❑ MT42709-1	Christina's Ghost	Betty Ren Wright	$2.75
❑ MT43461-6	The Dollhouse Murders	Betty Ren Wright	$2.75
❑ MT42319-3	The Friendship Pact	Susan Beth Pfeffer	$2.75
❑ MT43444-6	Ghosts Beneath Our Feet	Betty Ren Wright	$2.75
❑ MT40605-1	Help! I'm a Prisoner in the Library	Eth Clifford	$2.50
❑ MT42193-X	Leah's Song	Eth Clifford	$2.50
❑ MT43618-X	Me and Katie (The Pest)	Ann M. Martin	$2.75
❑ MT42883-7	Sixth Grade Can Really Kill You	Barthe DeClements	$2.75
❑ MT40409-1	Sixth Grade Secrets	Louis Sachar	$2.75
❑ MT42882-9	Sixth Grade Sleepover	Eve Bunting	$2.75
❑ MT41732-0	Too Many Murphys		
	Colleen O'Shaughnessy McKenna		$2.75
❑ MT41118-7	Tough-Luck Karen	Johanna Hurwitz	$2.50
❑ MT42326-6	Veronica the Show-off	Nancy K. Robinson	$2.75

Available wherever you buy books...or use the coupon below.

Scholastic Inc., P.O. Box 7502, 2932 East McCarty Street, Jefferson City, MO 65102

Please send me the books I have checked above. I am enclosing $_____ (please add $2.00 to cover shipping and handling). Send check or money order — no cash or C.O.D. s please.

Name_____

Address_____

City _____ State/Zip _____

Please allow four to six weeks for delivery. Offer good in the U.S.A. only.
Sorry, mail orders are not available to residents of Canada. Prices subject to change.

APP1089

America's Favorite Series

THE BABY-SITTERS CLUB®

by Ann M. Martin

Collect Them All!

The seven girls at Stoneybrook Middle School get into
all kinds of adventures...with school, boys, and, of course, baby-sitting!

☐ MG41588-3	Baby-sitters on Board! Super Special #1	$2.95
☐ MG41583-2	#19 Claudia and the Bad Joke	$2.75
☐ MG42004-6	#20 Kristy and the Walking Disaster	$2.75
☐ MG42005-4	#21 Mallory and the Trouble with Twins	$2.75
☐ MG42006-2	#22 Jessi Ramsey, Pet-sitter	$2.75
☐ MG42007-0	#23 Dawn on the Coast	$2.75
☐ MG42002-X	#24 Kristy and the Mother's Day Surprise	$2.75
☐ MG42003-8	#25 Mary Anne and the Search for Tigger	$2.75
☐ MG42419-X	Baby-sitters' Summer Vacation Super Special #2	$2.95
☐ MG42503-X	#26 Claudia and the Sad Good-bye	$2.95
☐ MG42502-1	#27 Jessi and the Superbrat	$2.95
☐ MG42501-3	#28 Welcome Back, Stacey!	$2.95
☐ MG42500-5	#29 Mallory and the Mystery Diary	$2.95
☐ MG42499-8	Baby-sitters' Winter Vacation Super Special #3	$2.95
☐ MG42498-X	#30 Mary Anne and the Great Romance	$2.95
☐ MG42497-1	#31 Dawn's Wicked Stepsister (February '90)	$2.95
☐ MG42496-3	#32 Kristy and the Secret of Susan (March '90)	$2.95
☐ MG42495-5	#33 Claudia and the Mystery of Stoneybrook (April '90)	$2.95
☐ MG42494-7	#34 Mary Anne and Too Many Boys (May '90)	$2.95
☐ MG42508-0	#35 Stacey and the New Kids on the Block (June '90)	$2.95

For a complete listing of all the Baby-sitter Club titles write to :
Customer Service at the address below.

Available wherever you buy books...or use the coupon below.

Scholastic Inc. P.O. Box 7502, 2932 E. McCarty Street, Jefferson City, MO 65102

Please send me the books I have checked above. I am enclosing $_____

(please add $2.00 to cover shipping and handling). Send check or money order–no cash or C.O.D.'s please.

Name_____

Address_____

City_____ State/Zip_____

Please allow four to six weeks for delivery. Offer good in U.S.A. only. Sorry, mail order not available to residents of
Canada.   Prices subject to change.   BSC 789